Jacked Up

HELEN JULIET

Jacked Up

Copyright © 2023 by Helen Juliet

Cover Design by Cate Ashwood

Trigger Warning

This book mentions the death of a lover due to AIDS-related illnesses as well as the death of a parent in a car crash. Both events happened in the past and the book does not go into graphic details on page.

This book also contains a consensual Dom/sub relationship between two adults with BDSM elements and aftercare.

CHAPTER 1

Jack

"Well, aren't you a sight for sore eyes, ya wee fecker."

I do my best not to flinch as Micky's hand slams into my back, almost making me spill my pint all over my hand and the small table I've been waiting at for over an hour. My drink sloshes but manages to stay within the confines of its glass, and therefore my glare is tempered toward the lanky bastard who drops into the empty seat opposite me.

"You're late," I grumble.

Micky scoffs and sips from his own beer before placing it down centrally on a fresh cardboard coaster with the pub's name and logo embossed onto it. "Like you have anywhere to be," he quips with a grin in that thick Scottish accent of his. It took me a month before I could understand half of what he was saying when we first met.

In some ways, that was a lifetime ago. In others, it feels like just yesterday I was a terrified nineteen-year-old being ushered into Her Majesty's Prison Lowsville.

I repress a shudder. Despite the reason for this clandestine meeting, there's no way I ever want to do time behind bars again. So I just need to make sure I don't get caught, hence reaching out to one of the few bastards who had my back during those two, dark years of my life.

Whilst I was serving time for a truly spectacular fuck up of a burglary, Michael Muir was doing a stretch for crimes of a far more technical nature. In fact, it hadn't been his first stint in jail, but it was to be his last.

The next time he hacked into MI5's security system just for laughs, they gave up and hired him.

I wouldn't recommend getting caught with a backpack full of diamond jewellery, but that stupid juvenile misstep did leave me with a list of very interesting phone numbers that I've made use of several times over the past decade. Once Micky 'The Matrix' Muir took me under his wing, I discovered a lot more blokes were willing to give me the time of day.

I look him up and down now. He's good-looking in a rugged, scrawny sort of way. Reddish-brown hair and a lopsided grin that he throws around freely. More tattoos than me, but that's only because he's had a decade more to work on his ink. I'll get there, I'm sure. We've never fucked—even I'm not that thick to complicate things like that—but I can see his attractiveness. I'm pretty sure that he charms his way out of as many situations as he hacks himself into.

Nope, he's more like an older brother to me. I'm not sure I always like him, but I can trust him to have my back.

Or to risk his neck when I decide that after eleven years, it's time to do something really fucking stupid again.

"You have what I need?" I ask.

He rolls his eyes and sips his pint again. "Wha'? No chit-chat for ya old pal? Don't I get to know the reasoning behind this harebrained scheme o' yours? You know I could lose mah job for this, and I really like mah job. It's where I get mah money from."

I purse my lips together and glance around. We're

currently huddled in a London East End pub on a Friday night, so it's packed with rowdy customers who don't give a shit what we're talking about. But I still feel vulnerable discussing what he's quite rightly labelled as 'this hare-brained scheme of mine' out in the open. I've spent the past decade mostly doing small grifts or cash-in-hand manual labour sort of jobs. I swore I'd never be involved in another heist again.

But this is personal. This is for my mum.

I shrug and avoid Micky's eyes. "That wanker took something from me. Men like him never get to suffer any consequences of their actions, all high and mighty in his fancy penthouse whilst we're here on the ground, trying just to make ends meet. Fuck him. He's going to feel it this time."

Micky narrows his gaze at me, and I try not to squirm. I am fully aware of how monumentally stupid this is, but that guy fucked over my *mum*. Just before *Christmas*. Who makes mass redundancies in November? Unfeeling wankers, that's who. She's going to be evicted from her home, and he's got five of them. I looked it up on the internet.

"You gonna hurt this man?" Micky asks.

"No!" I splutter a little too loudly, earning myself a couple of raised eyebrows. But people soon go back to their business, and I clear my throat before continuing to talk to Micky at a more reasonable level. "No, of course not. I just want him to *feel* something. I want to take something personal. Sentimental."

"Expensive," Micky adds with a smirk.

"Well, the point is to get paid, yeah," I mumble into my pint. I don't want my mum out on the streets in winter, after all. And I won't turn down the chance for some fast cash.

But sincerely, if I wanted to just rob the man, I could get Micky to hack into a company account somewhere and lift a hundred grand.

Felix Fagiolo probably wouldn't even notice that, though. It makes me sick.

No, I want him to know I was in his home, that I took something that mattered to him. And the timing is perfect because he's away in New York for a month for whatever reason. His penthouse here in London is literally sitting there empty, practically begging for me to sneak in and pinch whatever I want.

That's where Micky comes in.

Probably sensing my impatience, he fishes into the inside pocket of his bomber jacket and reveals three different key fobs, splaying his hand flat so I can see them all. "This one," he says, indicating the black bullet-shaped object with a red tip, "is for the front door of the building. It'll also operate the elevator. This one" —he points to the yellow-tipped fob— "is for his front door, and this one is for the safe." That one has a green tip. Okay, I can remember that. It's like traffic lights, working up from stop to go.

"Amazing," I say in a breathy voice, reaching out for them. But Micky suddenly closes his hand into a fist, hiding them away.

"I also found the blueprint ta the top three floors," he says, plucking a USB stick from a different pocket. "AKA this guy's shag pad. I figured you could use all the help you could get ta get where you're going fast."

Something akin to gratitude rushes through me. He might be a ruffian and a bit of a dickhead, but Micky is one of the few people in this world that looks out for me aside from my mum.

"Thanks," I say quietly but with appreciation.

He arches an eyebrow at me. "Dinna thank me yet, laddie. Mah cut is twenty percent."

I nod. "Yeah, I know. That's more than fair, since you're

sticking your neck out for me. But I need to fence whatever it is I manage to grab before paying you."

He hums. "Y'know I need some sort of guarantee, though. I'm not a fool. I need insurance. It's just good business practice."

"Right," I say slowly. "You get the part where I don't have any money right now, yeah? I gave it all to my mum to keep her going." It's not like I'm living in the lap of luxury, after all. I'm huddled up in a flat share in a room barely bigger than a postage stamp sharing a kitchen and bathroom with three other blokes and only having hot running water about thirty percent of the time.

He places a hand over his heart and sticks out his bottom lip in a display of less-than-sincere sympathy. "Well, aren't you an angel, hmm?" He drops his hand and smooths out his face. "But I want ta ensure you don't get silly when your pockets are full." He juts his chin at me. "Your jacket."

My blood runs cold, and I glance down at the leather jacket I've worn every day of my life since I regained my freedom.

My dad's jacket.

You see, there was a reason I lost my mind at nineteen and agreed to such a reckless job. When my dad was killed in a random stupid fucking car crash, I just sort of stopped caring. Stopped thinking straight. I was made of nothing but rage and grief. Prison, however, gave me a long time to think about what he'd want for me now he's gone, and throwing everything away wouldn't be it. Not to mention abandoning my mum.

I wear this jacket every day as a way of honouring the promise I since made to him. It's the only thing I have of his, and it's my way of feeling close to him.

Micky knows this.

"I don't…you can't…" I stammer.

He sighs. "Dinna ye look at me like I'm some sort of villain," he says, wagging his finger at me. "I'll keep it safe. But if I've got that, I *know* you'll come back ta me once the job is done." He sniffs and swirls his beer around in the glass. "I also know it'll give you the best incentive ta get your arse out of there and no' get caught."

"I won't get caught," I growl.

He shrugs. "Nobody ever *means* ta get caught, do they?" he says. "I just think this'll keep yer mind focused. I dinna want ta see you going back ta jail, laddie. Believe it or not, I give a shite about you, you wee fecker. So let's just get this over with. Three magic beans for yer da's jacket. Just until payday. All right?"

I swallow, looking at the fobs he's revealed in his palm once more. I suppose thinking of them as beans instead of bullets is tempting fate less. I'm certain from my research that Fagiolo won't have any kind of security guards, and guns are so rare here in the UK, but still...this isn't something I want to get shot for.

I rub the soft cuff of my jacket and bite my lip. Micky's right. If anything is going to motivate me to do a good job and make it out in one piece, it'll be to get this back. I sigh and nod in defeat.

"Deal," I say, keeping my voice firm despite how much it wants to waver. I might be thirty now, but in that moment with my old cellmate Micky, I can't help but feel like a dumb teenager again.

I just hope I don't regret this and ruin my life forever. But I have to *try*.

Felix Fagiolo is going to suffer, even just a little bit. And my family will make it through this Christmas without finding ourselves left out in the cold.

It's a simple plan. Really, what could go wrong?

CHAPTER 2

Jack

Now I get why Micky called the three fobs 'magic beans'. I'm standing at the base of 22-24 Cutter Street, or as it's apparently more affectionately known in the city, The Beanstalk. All the modern skyscrapers have cute names like that around here: The Cheese Grater, The Walkie-Talkie, The Gherkin. I've never paid much attention to this one before, so that's probably why I've never heard its more popular moniker.

Now it's got all my attention.

It's a tall and skinny building, and the balconies that jut out from all four sides at regular intervals all have luscious gardens overflowing them. From my research, I learned they were a result of some environmental scheme to improve air quality in the city. They kind of look like leaves, so I guess that's how the skyscraper got its nickname.

Nerves boil in my belly as I lick my lips and go over the plan again in my head. I've been sat at this café for an hour whilst I work up the courage to get on my feet and cross the road. Once I get through that front door, there's no going back.

At least, I hope I can get through the door. I trust implicitly that Micky wouldn't knowingly fuck me over. He's got a moral code about shit like that. But there are still a hundred things that could go wrong that I probably haven't even considered as well as all the ones I have.

But I know I don't really have a choice. My mum was barely living paycheque to paycheque as it was. This is a *good* plan. I just need to keep my head, and then I, she, and even Micky will be set up sweet for a long time to come.

She only needs a month or two to get back on her feet and find another job. Admin and office work is all she's ever done, but she's always struggled since computers came into the equation and now, with the arthritis, her fingers don't work as well as they should anymore. It's easy to see why companies would overlook her again and again for younger, more experienced employees.

I know there's something out there for her, though. Something that will make her happy. I do my best to help out, but I know she worries herself silly over my shenanigans. And if she's not busy, she just falls into that black hole where she misses my dad so badly she gets it in her head that she should just give up on this life and go join him in the next.

A lump threatens to rise in my throat, and I angrily swallow it down. Nope. Nuh-uh. That's not going to happen. She's *my* mum and I'm going to take care of her, no matter what. If I can pull off this caper, she'll be more than fine for years.

Time to stop procrastinating and get this done.

My overpriced cup of tea has already been paid for, so I gather up my rucksack and sling it over my shoulders. I debated bringing a bigger bag as I'm not really sure of what I'll be able to get my hands on once I'm inside Fagiolo's penthouse. But I figured if I kept things small and portable, it would be much easier to make a quick getaway.

Or even run for it.

No, it's not going to come to that. I have the three key fobs, and Micky wouldn't let me down. It's time to collect what's owed to my family, and that rich bastard is going to cough up whether he likes it or not.

I take a deep breath and pull the brim of my baseball cap down tighter over my head as I wait at the traffic lights to cross the road. I'm dressed all in black with a high-vis jacket over the top that I can ditch once the job is done. That, coupled with the very realistic-looking ID badge I cobbled together declaring I'm from a telecoms company that services the building, I'm really hoping people will just look right through me.

The lights change to green, and a swathe of people begin marching over to the other side of the street. I'm surrounded by city workers and tourists alike, every face I glance at wearing varying looks of concentration. I feel like everyone around me is on a mission, whether to get to a meeting on time or follow the right directions to a beloved monument.

Then there's me. Up to no good.

I've read a lot about people who get off on keeping secrets. Apparently, it's a real thrill to walk around knowing that nobody else is aware of what's going on in your head. That sounds kind of psychotic to me. I'm certainly not feeling any kind of glee or giddiness as I make myself stride up to the front entrance of The Beanstalk. I just feel a bit sick and dizzy.

"You're only doing this because you *have* to," I mutter to myself as I walk up to the building. And yeah, I know I don't *have* to do anything at all. I'm choosing to take revenge on the head honcho of the company who is trying its hardest to put my mum out on the streets. Mr Fagiolo has no clue who she is, I'm absolutely sure, let alone me.

But I'm like a dog with a bone. I've got the means and the determination. I'm going to pull this heist off, and whilst I'm not exactly going to write him a note informing him exactly who ripped him off, I'm definitely going to leave a few choice words on his mirror telling him he's a greedy bastard. I even pocketed a cheap crimson lipstick from the chemist just for the job.

I don't know if it's luck or what, but when I approach the door with the red-tipped fob in my hand, ready to go, a woman carrying an overflowing cardboard box slams into it from the other side, opening it for me. There's a large house plant getting its leaves in her face, but I can tell she's been crying. So I lurch forwards and grab the door, holding it so she and her belongings can make it outside intact.

"Thank you," she says with a sniffle and a weak smile.

Break up. It has to be. "You're better off without him," I say before I can stop my mouth from moving.

The woman barks out a laugh and nods at me. "You're probably right," she says as she hefts the box a little higher in her arms. "Thanks. Have a nice day."

"You, too," I murmur, watching her walk towards the tube station down the road.

I look down at the fob, not sure if I'm relieved or not that I didn't have to use it. I've got myself inside the building, but I still don't know whether or not my magic beans are working. I resist the urge to tug at my hat again in case I draw attention to it. But it's hopefully doing its job and hiding my face from any security cameras in the building or on the street outside, for that matter. There are cameras everywhere in London.

I chew my lip and look around the busy lobby. People are coming and going from all directions, which isn't surprising considering the bottom two-thirds of the floors are occupied by businesses. Only the top fifteen to twenty floors are residential, but they all cost an insane amount to buy.

The penthouse, obviously, is the most obscene of them all.

I take a deep breath and remember my cover story. I'm meant to be here. I'm working. So I walk with purpose over to the elevators, nodding at the security guard as he glances my way. I see his eyes flick to my forged ID lanyard, then look away again, clearly bored out of his mind. Right, good, excellent. *Just keep putting one foot in front of the other*, I think firmly to myself.

Unfortunately—or fortunately—there's a crowd of people who push into the lift at the same time as me, and only one of them needs to use a fob to operate it. I swallow my nerves as best I can and slip the red-tipped bean back into my pocket. I guess we'll find out if the yellow one works soon enough.

The climb seems to take forever, with people exiting every couple of floors. Once there's a little more room, I move over to the console and press the button at the very top for the penthouse.

Nothing happens.

I try it again.

"You need one of these, darling," an older lady says, wiggling a familiar-looking fob at me. Hers is just plain black. Before I can reach into my pocket and show her that I do in fact have one, she leans over and touches hers to the pad instead. "There you go. Try that again."

I grin sheepishly and do as she says. Sure enough, the topmost button suddenly glows. "Thank you," I say genuinely, although I kind of want to tell her off for being too trusting. Doesn't she know there are thieving arseholes out there?

Gradually, more and more people filter out until it's just

me left by myself as the elevator races up the last few floors. My palms are sweating, so I rub them against my cargo trousers. I can't afford any fuck-ups.

"He deserves this," I say out loud through gritted teeth. The faceless billionaire who treats his employees like shit. Honestly, I couldn't even find a picture of this Fagiolo guy. He just sits up here in his ivory tower, playing god with the lives of us mere mortals.

Time to bring him back down to earth.

When the elevator dings and the doors slide open, I gird myself and march right over to the one and only door on the small landing. The penthouse. The yellow fob feels hot where it's pressed so tightly between my finger and thumb, and my heart is thumping against my ribcage like it's going to explode from my chest. I've made it this far. I've got to make it inside. I can't fail now. I don't pause. I just raise my hand and thrust the small black bean at the wall pad…

And the door opens.

I stumble backwards in shock, looking between my hand and the blinking green light. The door hasn't actually physically opened, but I heard it click. So I grab for the handle before it can change its mind.

Yep. It really is open.

I try and regulate my breathing as I push the door inwards and take a careful step inside. *Fuck my life.* I've done it.

Well, not quite. I still have to manage the actual robbery part. But I've got my foot in the door, literally. I close it with a quiet little click, then step farther inside this insane home.

It takes me a few seconds to realise that my jaw is hanging open as I take in the floor-to-ceiling windows. The penthouse is three storeys, but the second and third floors don't extend all the way to the edge, finishing in balconies over my head, meaning that the windows tower several metres above me. The view of London is breathtaking. The nearby skyscrapers feel as if they're waving to me through the clouds. I can also see The Shard just over the river and even a glimpse of Tower Bridge, split halfway open to allow a ship to pass through on the Thames.

The penthouse itself is all white and chrome finishings with black furniture. Some kind of modern white sculpture hangs in several pieces from overhead beams, filling in the space between the two balconies that run the length of the apartment and the glass. There's an empty fireplace and a TV on the wall so enormous it could be a cinema screen, currently black and lifeless.

The only colour that cuts through the monochrome is the abundance of red roses bunched together in cut crystal vases all over what I assume to be the living room space. I think of my mum's cramped lounge with its worn, mismatching furniture, collection of tatty blankets, and about a hundred photos of me from when I was growing up. Hers and Dad's wedding photos are still proudly on display in a faded frame, the gold paint peeling at the edges if you look close enough.

I get a pang in my chest so hard it's almost painful. That's a home to me, but I feel awful because I can't deny that there's something about this lavish place that I find beautiful as well. It's totally devoid of personality, of course, but I always knew I'd have to dig a little deeper to find that.

Unsurprisingly, Felix Fagiolo has hidden who he truly is behind a locked steel door.

The safe.

Thanks to Micky's blueprint, I know exactly which direction to sprint silently in. For a second, I pause as I'm met with a wall hosting an enormous canvas that just looks like a toddler has splattered different colours of paint onto it, and yet I'm quite sure is worth millions. But then I have a thought and begin running my hands along both sides, one after another. Sure enough, with a good tug, the left side starts to swing outward, revealing a large safe door hidden behind.

I gulp and try not to break into a sweat. This is okay. I was expecting nothing less. I can do this—or at least I used to be able to. I shake out my limbs and pull myself together. Micky got me the key fob, that's the most important thing. It's like a handprint and an eye scan combined. Everything else my nifty little gadgets can take care of.

Still, it takes far longer than I'd hoped to get the mechanisms of the damn thing turning and clunking, and even though I know I'm alone, I'm still freaking out at the noise and how long it's taking.

"Come on, come on," I mutter, watching as the numbers flick on my reader, the computer doing a million maths calculations in mere seconds. Once I have the code (that changes every thirty seconds) I'll just use the fob and *voilà!* I'll be in.

Simple.

I've still chewed my lip practically raw by the time the sequences have been completed, and I feel like my heart is literally in my throat. I take a deep, shuddery breath. This is the moment of truth. Micky might have managed to get me inside the penthouse, but I don't even know if the front door key would have worked.

I think of my mum, sitting alone in the cold and the dark, and squeeze my eyes shut before thrusting the green-tipped fob at the keypad.

Nothing happens.

I crack one eyelid open just a fraction, too afraid to really know if I've failed. I daren't breathe.

Then there's one last almighty clank, and this time the door does swing open to greet me.

I let out a giddy laugh. I can't believe it! I've done it! And what a treasure trove awaits me as I step over the threshold. I'm not even entirely sure what I'm looking at, but I can see artwork, jewels, vases, and sculptures. An enormous golden harp takes up most of one of the walls. It's like Aladdin's cave. Not to mention, there is an entire wall of drawers that I assume are full of cash and bonds and stuff. I see collections of fountain pens and fancy watches, but that's not what ultimately draws me in closer.

There's a shallow glass display cabinet that's over a metre high and probably two metres in width. It's lined with a bold red velvet—the same colour as the roses—and inside are row upon row of antique coins.

Naturally. He's so rich he even collects *money*. My lip curls in disgust, and I know exactly what I want to take from him.

Everything I can possibly carry.

There's just one teeny, tiny little problem.

"Can I *help* you with something?" a booming voice comes from behind me.

CHAPTER 3

Felix

I KNOW I SHOULD BE EXTREMELY PISSED OFF. THREATENED, even. But when you're as big of a bastard as I am, it takes a lot to rattle me.

I cross my arms and take in the horrified-looking man currently frozen in the middle of my safe. He's small—well, most people are smaller than me. But he's got to be barely five foot five with slim shoulders and hips. Black hair tucked under a baseball cap. His skin is pale, although his cheeks are at present turning a very blotchy shade of red, and he has several tattoos I can see peeking out from his collar and sleeves.

I note the high-vis jacket and what I assume to be an entirely fake ID badge he's got slung around his neck, and I remind myself again that I should be furious. This fucker has broken into my *home* and is clearly trying to *rob* me.

Instead, I'm just kind of impressed.

"Well?" I ask.

"Huh?" he squeaks in reply.

I force myself not to chuckle. I can't see all of his face

under that cap, but I can't help but feel like this man is pretty cute.

Wow—and the award for the most inappropriate thought goes to Felix Fagiolo. I'll have to add it to the shelf with all the others gathering dust.

"Well?" I repeat. "Can I help you with something?"

I don't know why, but I'm kind of enjoying playing with him. Watching him squirm. As soon as I heard noises coming from downstairs, I should have called the police. However, maybe it's a tragic sign of how starved I've been of human company lately, but I'm having rather a lot of fun teasing this poor sod.

He licks his lips, his breathing shallow and wild like a frightened animal. I wait patiently to see what he's going to do next. After all, I'm stood in the doorway, blocking his escape route. Apparently, though, that's not going to be enough to deter him from trying to make a getaway.

He suddenly lunges forwards and grabs one of my first edition Charles Dickens novels and flings it at my head. I lurch backwards in surprise and bat it away, but it's the distraction he needs to make a run for it.

Sadly for him, I played rugby my entire life until my knees gave out. My reflexes kick in, and I dart to the right, blocking his escape path once again, forcing him to bounce off my chest.

Right into my display cabinet.

It's like watching a pinball ricochet around one of those games you used to get down the pub. He pushes himself off the cabinet, only to hit the wall of safety deposit boxes, then careens back into the table in the middle, shoving it back into the display cabinet and dislodging several loose-standing items in the process. I dart forwards and snatch a vase before it can smash to the ground, but watch as everything else goes crashing downwards, hoping nothing gets too bent out of shape.

My intruder loses his footing and slams back on his arse, blinking in shock. But then his head snaps at the same time as mine in response to the creaking and cracking noises coming from the display cabinet. I flinch, unable to do anything as the base gives way, and my entire coin collection slides loose, the protective glass shattering upon impact.

The guy throws his arms up to protect himself from any flying shards, and then an eery quiet settles around us both. The only sounds I can hear are his short, panicky breaths as he stares incredulously at the mess he's caused.

I exhale, puffing out my cheeks and scratching the back of my neck.

"Right, then," I say before turning on my heels and walking towards the kitchen.

There is only one way to deal with how I'm feeling in this present moment, and it comes in liquid form.

I'm still not furious, but my mirth has dimmed. I place the vase I rescued on the counter, fetch my preferred, hefty cut crystal glass from its place of pride, and pour myself two fingers of Irish whiskey.

I shake my head before taking a sip. There I was, worrying about facing yet another boring day by myself. I can't really complain now. My afternoon certainly has got a *lot* more interesting.

Scuffing noises alert me that my little burglar is probably on the move, and sure enough, he soon peeks his head out from the safe. His eyebrows shoot up as he registers me in the open-plan kitchen, and I raise my glass in a salute at him. He gives another (definitely not cute) squeak before legging it down the hall towards the front door.

"Going somewhere?" I ask lazily. I can't stop my lips from

curling in amusement as I watch him skid to a halt and throw his entire body weight into yanking the door handle.

It doesn't budge.

He was probably too busy wrestling his way into my safe to notice me come out a few minutes ago and secure the premises. I'm not sure how he came across the means to be able to break his way into here, but it takes a different key as well as a code to open the door from the inside.

He's trapped.

And as he slowly turns around and gapes at me, I know that he knows that.

I flash a grin at him. "Leaving so soon? But we were just starting to get to know each other."

"Let me *out!*" he spits. He's got fighting spirit, I'll give him that.

I shrug, unbothered. "I was planning on keeping you here whilst I call the police," I tell him truthfully, getting a small amount of satisfaction when the colour drains from his face. I mean, what did he think was going to happen? He's lucky they're not here already.

But that does beg the question of myself. *Why* haven't I called them yet? I've had plenty of chances. I lick my lips, savouring the spicy tang of the whiskey, and look my little thief up and down again.

I should probably be concerned with how intrigued I am by him. I'm fully aware of how infrequently I've been venturing out from this flat of late. Human company has become a rarity. Even the people I video-call with are almost always employees.

Now I find myself with this strange chap dropped into my lap, and I'm *fascinated.* How did he get in here? Why is he here? Obviously, he was hoping to liberate me of several of my more expensive collectables and earn himself a payday, but why me and my things? Surely there had to be easier targets.

My intruder crosses his arms and glares mulishly at me. "Go on, then," he barks. "Call the police. Get it over with. You've clearly got me at your mercy."

It is very, *very* bad how his words shoot directly to my dick. It's been a long time since I've had any man at my mercy, and I bet this guy would be an absolute alley cat between the sheets.

Except he's probably not even into men, and—*hello*—I caught him red-handed trying to rob me, for fuck's sake.

Yeah…my dick doesn't seem to give a shit. It's got my eyes lingering on his pretty pink lips, thinking how they might look stretched around my cock.

So not the issue at hand, Fagiolo.

I sigh and take another sip of my whiskey, aware that I'm going to make a really stupid decision but apparently unable to stop myself anyway. "I haven't called anyone," I inform him, watching carefully as his eyes narrow in suspicion at me. I don't blame him. He's probably wondering what the hell I'm going to say next.

That makes two of us.

I glance back towards the safe, and an idea forms in an instant. I'm not sure if it's a *good* idea or not, but fuck it. For whatever reason, I don't want to hand this guy over to the authorities. It feels mean spirited. He so nearly got away with his little caper and probably would have without a hitch if I'd been in New York like I was supposed to be.

"Here's the deal," I announce, walking around the kitchen counter into the main living space. That way, I can see him better where he's still lingering by the front door. I want him to look me in the eyes when I make this proposition.

"Yeah?" he says defiantly.

"You stay here and fix what you wrecked just now," I tell

him. "You do that, and I'll let you go without any fuss or involving law enforcement."

"You what?" he splutters.

"Clean up your mess and walk away, or I call the police," I say plainly with another shrug.

He licks his lips (and I *don't* look at them), frowning. "What's to stop me from just legging it?"

"The door is locked, and it's going to stay that way."

He scoffs. "So you're kidnapping me?"

I try and fail not to grin. He's fucking *adorable*. I haven't felt anything stir in me like this for years. I know this isn't a date, but still, it's nice to know I'm not completely dead below the waist.

"I'm giving you an opportunity to make amends," I say. "You *did* break into my home, remember? Actions have consequences."

At that, he really does bark out a laugh and roll his eyes. "That's fucking *rich* coming from you, you son of a bitch. Let me out of here, *right now.*"

"Or you'll what?" I ask calmly. I make a mental note to come back to that 'coming from you' comment, but right now, I have other more pressing issues.

His mouth opens and closes like a goldfish, and I do my best not to smirk. Yeah, he's not thick. He's just a scrapper. He doesn't want to go down without a fight.

Just how I like them.

"To be clear," I say as I swirl my drink, looking at the amber liquid before glancing up at him through my eyelashes and quirking a brow. "I'm offering you house and board whilst you complete a task for me. That doesn't sound so bad, does it? I think it's a *much* better deal than whatever prison sentence you're bound to get."

He grits his jaw and blinks several times, his hands gripping onto the straps of his backpack. He knows I'm right.

He's like a worm, wriggling on a hook. I can't deny how hot that makes me under the collar.

"You want me to pick up all the coins?" he says uncertainly.

I chuckle lightly. "To start with. I need everything else picked up and inspected for damage as well, once you've cleaned up every splinter of glass, of course. I'm sure it won't take long. No more than a couple of days."

"A couple of days!" he shrieks.

I throw him a sincerely amused look. "As opposed to a couple of *decades* behind bars."

I'm just guessing, but from the way his face goes slack, I think I'm right in my assumption that this isn't his first offence. It can't be with how competent he is, but I'd wager he's been caught before, and therefore, getting pinched for this would come with a much higher penalty.

"I hate to blow my own trumpet," I say, and he makes a disgusted noise that I ignore. But yeah, this guy knows me on some kind of level and apparently has a very low opinion of me. "However, I'm offering you a ridiculously good deal here. I could just hand you over to the authorities and walk away, never having to think about you again. But you clean up your mess, and *you* can be the one to walk away and never think about me again. Is there even really a question here?"

He balls up his fists and glares at me from under the brim of that baseball cap. "Why?" he demands. "Why not just call the police."

I sigh and look at the last little bit of my drink. "Because life is too fucking short," I mutter, "and I believe in second chances. No one should have to lose everything just because of one dumb mistake."

His Adam's apple bobs, and he screws up his eyes. For a few moments, I just watch him, holding my breath, strangely hanging on tenterhooks.

Eventually, he opens his eyes and glowers at me.

"Fine," he spits out. *"Deal."*

"Excellent," I say cheerfully whilst something a little dastardly unfurls in my belly.

I promise myself not to cross any lines…but I have a feeling this is going to be *fun.*

CHAPTER 4

Jack

I'M NOT SURE WHAT THE HELL IS GOING ON. I FEEL SCARED TO even breathe too heavily in case something shifts and this giant fucker decides he's going to call the police after all.

And man, he is *big*.

I know I'm small, but I've always thought of myself as one of those scrappy little terrier dogs that'll go for your ankles if you try and fuck with them. I might be tiny, but I'm still tough. But this guy? Fucking hell. He's got to be over a foot taller than me—maybe even a foot and a half? Could he be seven feet tall? And he's not skinny, either. His shoulders look like he rips through shirts like a superhero, and his thighs could smash watermelons like a hippopotamus's jaws. I bet he struggles getting through doors, and *that's* why he's such a recluse.

I also can't help but imagine fleetingly how fucking amazing a body like that could feel crushing you into a mattress.

I give myself a little shake and shove that line of thinking firmly to the back of my mind. The man is essentially kidnapping me, and here my cock is jumping to attention, helpfully informing me that if ever there was a man who was designed to be climbed like a tree, it's this one.

It doesn't help that he seems genuinely delighted that I've agreed to stay with him and try to put back together everything I just completely fucked up in his safe. How starved for company is this guy? He didn't even seem that angry that he was being robbed.

Am I that unimpressive? Doesn't he take me seriously at all?

Fuck it. Now I've agreed to stay and pick up all his stupid coins, there's got to be a way I can find to pocket something small without him noticing. If he's really going to let me go after I'm done, there's a chance I could still get *some* money out of it.

Even if it's only enough to pay back Micky. There's no way in hell I'm letting him keep my dad's leather jacket. Nope.

But now I have no idea what the hell I'm supposed to do. This is extremely awkward. I'm essentially under house arrest. Where am I supposed to go? Sleep? God, as if I could sleep when I'm being held against my will. Is he even going to feed me?

"What now, then?" I snap irritably.

Don't get me wrong—him not calling the police is like some sort of miracle. I'd be completely and utterly fucked if I got arrested again. I'd be lucky if I only got a decade. Chances are I'd be in there until well into my forties.

Fagiolo finishes his drink and sets the thick-cut crystal tumbler on the kitchen counter. "I think it's probably a good idea for you to give me your phone. That way, it's just the two of us and nobody's getting the police involved, no matter what."

I blanch. "I'm not giving you my phone," I rasp, taking a

step backwards, even though I know by now that the door really is locked.

He gives me a curious look. "You seem to be struggling to remember whose house this is—who's in charge. Surely you understand that I can't let you keep a smart phone. Your track record with me is only five minutes long and I hate to break it to you, but you haven't come across as very trustworthy."

He flashes me a smile, lines crinkling around his eyes. I'm pretty certain I read that he was in his mid-to-late forties, but I can't remember exactly now. If so, he's in good shape for a guy approaching fifty. He's probably got a private gym in here, that wouldn't surprise me.

For fuck's sake, Jack! I think angrily to myself. *Get your head out of the clouds and focus!*

He's still looking at me like I amuse him. Admittedly, that's better than if he was looking like he wanted to punch me, but at least that I could understand. I broke into his home, and he seems to just think it's kind of funny.

It's really not funny.

"How do I know you won't hurt me?" I say, mortified when my voice cracks. But I don't like being helpless. I do all right in day-to-day life, but when I was locked up, Micky's people couldn't look out for me *all* the time. I've taken a few beatings.

A couple of times it got much, *much* worse.

Something changes in Fagiolo's expression, and he's looking at me with concern as he takes a step forward. Instinctively I throw my fists up and take a step back, even though I'm sure there's very little I could do if he decided to do something awful.

"Whoa, hey," he says, holding up his enormous hands. "I swear to you you're in no danger. This really isn't a trick. I don't know why you're here...but I have the feeling I've already hurt you in some way, and for that I'm truly sorry. I won't hurt you again. You have my word."

Something sad and pitiful pops in me, like an already half-deflated balloon. He's not supposed to apologise. He's not supposed to be nice and sound so completely sincere. He's the *devil.* His soulless company has ruined my mum's life and hundreds of others right before Christmas.

I wanted to make him pay. I never expected the satisfaction of an apology, and now I'm left holding it, a limp and pathetic thing, and I'm not sure where to put it or how to feel about it.

I certainly don't know what to reply to him in this moment. I'm not saying 'thank you', that's for sure. He doesn't get off that easily. But he's just *so* not what I was expecting from a supposedly evil, reclusive billionaire. I'd built him up like a movie villain in my mind, and now...

Now he's worried that he's hurt me in the past and made me scared in the present. Although he has assured me that if we can work through this agreement, I won't have to fear him in the future.

Fine. The quicker I can get through this, the quicker we can part ways and forget this ever happened. But I'm still not comfortable handing over my phone and leaving myself completely vulnerable to him.

"What if I need to call someone in an emergency?" I say, stalling as he gets closer to me. He's creeping like he's approaching a wounded animal, but I suppose I am just that to a certain extent. I'm certainly panicking as I press my backpack up to the locked front door. "What if I need help?"

"I can call someone if you need help," Fagiolo assures me.

I scowl. "What if I need help from *you?* People are going to know I'm missing, you know. They'll worry if I drop off the face of the Earth."

He tilts his head and gives me a small smile. I hate that he obviously pities me. The silly little man he caught trying to rob him. He doesn't respect me. I'm like…a social experiment to him.

"I get the feeling," he says, "that a man such as yourself could text those near to him, letting them know that he's got something going on. That he won't be contactable for the next few days, and they won't be that surprised. Why don't you get your phone out and send something like that to whoever might fret over your absence, and I can watch to make sure there's no funny business."

"Why do you have to watch?" I spit out, hating the idea of him snooping on me.

He lets out a sorrowful chuckle. "You do remember that you—"

"—broke into your house," I finish for him with an unhappy grunt. I hate that he's being so reasonable about being the victim. He could be ruining my life right now and instead he's giving me a chance to make amends.

I low-key despise him for that. But I also begrudgingly have to acknowledge that's a pretty decent thing for him to do. I didn't want to admit that he could be anything other than a hundred percent bad. What he did was so callous. I don't want to like a single thing about him.

However, I can't ignore that by not calling the police, he's literally saving my life. I'm not sure I'd survive another prison cell.

So if I have to be incarcerated somewhere, even for a little while, I really need to dredge up some gratitude that it's going to be here in the lap of luxury, looking out through the clouds onto the city I love, the city I call home.

I glance up and realise that he's towering over me. My heart races as I feel the solid door behind me, and in that moment, I've never felt so trapped in my life. But his smile is kind and patient. He nods and raises his eyebrows at me, telling me that what happens next is entirely up to me.

I swing my empty backpack around and open the main zipper. Then I jostle it so I can open the pocket in the back where I'd put my personal belongings for safekeeping during the now-aborted heist. This is my everyday bag, so it already had keys for my place and my mum's, as well as some emergency cash, my tube pass, condoms, painkillers and…

And my emergency meds.

My heart lurches in my chest. I could tell him I have to take daily meds but lie and say I don't have any here. Then he'd *have* to let me go, right?

But would he have no choice but to call the police, then? There is absolutely nothing stopping him from reporting the very real crime I just committed against him. The only reason I'm still here is because he's choosing to show me mercy.

I bite my lip and quickly scan the pill packet. I keep these here in case I go home with someone and don't want to risk skipping a dose the morning after. There's about a week's worth. Patching up that stupid coin display can't possibly take that long, can it?

Not really sure if I'm being insane or not, I move my hand past the tablets and get my phone instead, unlocking it with my fingerprint and slinging the backpack over my shoulder once more.

"Who do you need to text?" he asks, moving around to my side so he can see my screen. He's so *close*. I could just lean in and…

And what? *Snuggle?* I really need to get a grip.

It feels horribly vulnerable for him to be looking at my lock screen of the photo I took of me and Mum on her birthday this year. But I guess I violated his home sanctuary, so getting a peek at my phone is probably only fair.

"Um, my mum," I say, waving the phone a little to indicate that's who he's looking at. "And my friend M—" I clear my throat, catching myself before I throw Micky under the bus. "My friend," I just repeat lamely.

"Your boyfriend?" he asks casually, and I almost drop the phone.

As a general rule, I try not to jump to any conclusions about people. But I'm pretty confident that a straight man of his age would ask if I had a girlfriend as a default. Or if he was open-minded maybe ask if I had a partner, keeping it gender neutral.

But he specifically asked if I had a *boyfriend*.

"N-no boyfriend," I say, clutching my phone so it doesn't tip out of my hand after all. We're huddled so close together in this short entrance hall I'm not sure what would happen if I had to bend over and pick something up.

"Just a friend," Fagiolo clarifies. He's still got that kind, patient air to his voice that I'm sure I don't deserve. Like I'm a little kitten he's picked off the street to help.

I want to lash out and push him away, but I don't. Because there's a small part of my heart that fucking *aches* to be looked after by anyone at all.

Of course my mum loves me and cares for me. But since Dad died, I feel like I'm the parent and I've had to keep everything together to make sure she's the one being supported. It's pathetic how I want to gravitate towards the first scrap of kindness that's come my way in so many years.

I hum instead of answering him and quickly open up my messages, finding the chat with my mum.

Hey! I've got a few things going on right now, so probably going to drop off the grid for a few days. No need to worry.

I copy Fagiolo's suggestion almost word for word because he's right. With my dodgy dealings, sometimes I do just go AWOL from time to time. As much as I try and keep to legitimate jobs, there are times when I need to go off the books and help move stolen goods or something just to make ends meet, and the fewer people who know about it, the better.

However, I add a smiley face emoji at the end of my message because I really don't want her to worry. Then I copy and paste it into my more recent chat with Micky, doing it as fast as I can so Fagiolo can't properly read our previous messages. Micky's last communication was wishing me good luck. It doesn't say specifically with what, but *I* know it was to come here and rob the man currently standing beside me.

"Happy?" I ask as I hold down the power button and turn the thing off. That way I won't have to worry about charging it whilst I'm here, and he's less likely to try and snoop around it. In theory, he'd need my fingerprint or passcode to access it, but I still feel better as I hand it over.

"Ecstatic," he says, flashing me that grin of perfect teeth again.

He takes the phone from my grasp, our fingers brushing ever so slightly, and I do my best not to shiver. I'm still not entirely sure what's going on here, but it's certainly not anything like *that*.

"Do you mind if I look through your bag?" he asks me.

"Yes," I say with a scowl as I lean back and press it against the door. "What for? It's basically empty." *Because I never got around to the robbery part of this wacky adventure.*

He still just looks amused at me. "To check you don't have any weapons. I'm sure it won't be an issue, seeing as we're friends and everything now. But it would ease my mind."

I grind my teeth, on the verge of snapping at him for being a total arsehole. But it's actually a pretty reasonable request. Guns might be extremely hard to come by in this country, but I could easily have pepper spray or, hell, a bloody kitchen knife.

Seeing as I have none of those things, I wordlessly thrust the still open bag towards him, my expression mutinous. He happily takes it from me and has a quick scan of the contents. As I'd already established, there's nothing in the main part, just my few personal items in the back pocket.

He doesn't comment on them, just hands the bag back to me. "And could you turn out your trouser pockets?"

I think the fact he's being so fucking cheerful about it all is grating on my nerves. But I bite my tongue and do as he says. There's the receipt from my tea earlier, the fobs, and…

And my lucky penny.

I bite my lip and study his face, but he doesn't seem to care about any of those things either. None of them could stab him, after all. So he just shrugs and nods. "Thank you."

My heart is beating fast as I slip them away again. It's ironic after seeing the impressive collection of coins I just scattered all over the floor in a sea of glass. They're probably worth thousands—maybe millions. My penny is barely worth its own value. But to me, it's priceless.

I was so stunned a few years back to find a coin still in circulation from 1993 that I held onto it. It's accidentally been in the wash a few times, but it's kind of a miracle that I've never lost it. Holding a coin from the year I was born made me feel strange—in a good way. I don't know why it's so precious to me, not really. But I'm relieved that he's let me put it back in my pocket along with the other items.

He doesn't comment on the fobs. I guess he either doesn't realise what they are or knows precisely and just doesn't care. Either way, I feel oddly glad to have passed his inspection. There's a small amount of guilt as well. I never intended to hurt him physically, and it unnerves me that he thought I might. Well, hopefully he can feel confident after looking through my stuff.

"So…what now?" I ask, genuinely unsure.

He slips my phone into his trouser pocket and shrugs mischievously. "I suppose you get to work...and I supervise."

I don't know why I have to repress another shudder at his words, but I do. *He's going to keep an eye on me so I don't do exactly what I'm planning and still try and rob him,* I tell myself firmly. *He's not watching me in a pervy way.*

Because that would be bad. I wouldn't want him watching me like that.

Right?

CHAPTER 5
Felix

IT TOOK A WHILE FOR MY LITTLE THIEF TO RELAX ENOUGH TO take off his high-vis, lanyard, and overshirt. His hat was the last thing to be removed, like he was protecting himself as long as he could, but I'm glad it's gone. I can finally see his pretty green eyes.

Now he's just in his black cargo trousers and a tight-fitting T-shirt, which shows that he might be small, but he's still got a decent amount of muscle on him. Physically, he doesn't look like a man who's afraid of a bit of manual labour.

However, he is gritting his teeth as I hand him a dustpan and brush, clearly still not entirely impressed with his new and exciting captivity. He has seen reason, though. Better this than getting arrested for breaking and entering, not to mention the property damage and attempted theft. But it amuses me that he's still putting up the tiniest bit of a fight.

It would be boring if he didn't.

"Okay, mate," I say as I hold up a tablet I've retrieved from the kitchen. Luckily, I had thoroughly photographed the contents of my safe for insurance purposes, so I've got detailed records of how it needs to be put back together. "This folder has pictures of every single coin. They all have to be accounted for. They can be set back into the velvet display case, and once things are a bit tidier in here, we can think about replacing the glass front."

He grunts, scowling at the photos I'm currently flicking through. I'm not a fool. Something tells me that he's still planning on trying to swipe something from me, and I'd really rather that didn't happen. If I supervise him closely enough, hopefully it won't give him the opportunity to do something he'll regret.

He probably just sees an overabundance of wealth. But everything in this vault is precious to me. It tells a story or has a history. Yes, some things, like the fountain pens, are an investment. They're like a kind of currency that I can sell if necessary. But they also remind me of my mother, who lovingly hand-wrote letters to all her friends around the world until she passed.

I'm perfectly aware that I'm trusting my treasures to a man who half an hour ago was trying to rob me of them. But I honestly hope that we've come to a place of at least fragile respect. If not that, then he understands that I've got him over a barrel. Yes, I'm risking him taking something from me that I care about deeply. But if he genuinely pisses me off, then I won't have any issues sending him off to New Scotland Yard.

I don't want it to come to that, though. I'm already getting a little bit fond of him.

He puffs out his cheeks and looks at the glittering mess of glass all over the floor. "I guess I could start by picking out the coins so they don't accidentally get swept up," he says in a defeated tone.

I clap him on his shoulder, pleased with how he staggers

on his feet. I know I'm a bastard, but I like the feel of him under my hand.

"Up to you, mate."

"I'm not..." he begins with a tut, then flashes me an irritable look. "I'm not your mate."

I shrug and let him go, knowing that's perfectly true. I secretly hope I might get to know him a little after this forced time together, but that's slightly crazy on my part. I could go out in the real world and make friends. I don't need to hold burglars hostage.

But people out there...they only see my money. My power. My size. It gets exhausting trying to make real connections with people, because quite frankly, they often look up to me like I'm some kind of god.

This fellow is mostly looking at me with contempt, and it's a refreshing kind of honesty.

"What should I call you, then?" I ask.

He narrows his eyes at me for a moment, but then his shoulders sag a little, and I can feel some of the fight blowing out of him. Good. That means I'm wearing him down.

"Jack," he says before turning and crouching down, inspecting the floor to begin his hunt for my precious coins.

I place the tablet on the table in the middle of the room and watch him, wondering if Jack is his real name. Something tells me from the way he gave up just then that it is.

Don't get me wrong, I would have been more than happy to keep playing tug of war a little longer. It was getting my blood rushing. But there's a part of me that wants to skip all that and try to get to know this young man better. I want to understand what makes him tick.

I want to discover why he's here in the first place.

"Nice to meet you, Jack," I say pleasantly.

He scoffs and glares at me over his shoulder. "Yeah, okay."

"I'm Felix," I offer, not put off by his grumpy mood. He

can sulk all he wants. He made the decision to try and steal from me, so he can hardly be angry at the consequences.

"I know who you are," he says frostily. He doesn't look at me, instead carefully plucking the red velvet display case out from the debris and giving it a gingerly shake. It looks like a wide set of tiny stairs with custom-made indents for each of the coins to sit in.

I look forward to my new friend Jack having to work out exactly which coin goes where. That's not going to be a nightmare at all.

"You know who I am, don't you?" I say, leaning against the wall and crossing my arms over my chest.

"Well, yeah," he says with his back still to me. "I did do my research before coming here."

I shake my head, though, not convinced. "No, you knew who I was before you planned this robbery. You didn't come here to steal anything in particular. You came here to rob *me*, to hurt *me*." I lick my lips, considering my next words. "Because I was right, wasn't I? I don't know the particulars, but somehow I've hurt you already. Or at least my company has."

He just grunts again as he starts to fish out coins from the mess. I grimace. Technically, none of those metals should be touched by human hands. But also, with all that glass everywhere, he's in danger of injuring himself.

"Hang on a second," I say, interrupting our important conversation. Because I really want to know how he knows me—or *thinks* he knows me—but I don't want him to—

"Fuck!" he cries, snatching his hand back and cradling it to his chest.

That. I didn't want him to do that.

"Oh shit, let me see," I say, immediately dashing to his side.

He hisses like an alley cat, but I ignore him as I crouch

down and pull at his wrist so I can look at the cut. He's caught the edge of his palm between his thumb and index finger. Bright red blood is already sliding over his skin, but it looks like a clean cut and not too deep.

"Well, that got off to a bad start, didn't it?" I say apologetically. "And I was just about to offer you some protective gloves. Come on, let's get you patched up. Then maybe I can feed you before sending you back in there. It's going to be a fairly involved task. No point in trying to rush it."

I stand up and help him to his feet, whether he wants me to or not. His small wrists feel so good with my fingers wrapped around them. I have to make my thoughts behave as I start leading him towards the kitchen.

"Are you getting off on humiliating me?" he grumbles.

I can't help but burst out laughing. I'm doing my very best to not get off on *something*, all right, but that's not it.

"I'm just trying to take care of you, my little indentured thief. You'll be no good at restoring my coin collection if your hands are all mangled."

He huffs angrily as I get him to sit on a stool at my breakfast bar. I switch on the tap, and he automatically sticks his hand underneath it, rinsing off the blood and, hopefully, any glass fragments that might have snuck into the gash.

"You're not…" he utters as I take the seat next to him with my first aid kit. He grits his teeth and shakes his head, looking away as I put on some latex gloves before inspecting the wound. Like I'd hoped, I can't see any foreign bodies there, and the bleeding is already slowing. A decent plaster should sort this out.

"Not what?" I prompt as I pat the area dry.

I get the plaster attached to his skin, and he still hasn't answered, so I think he's not going to. That's fine. He's a prickly little thing and obviously has a story to tell. I'd guess it's probably not all sunshine and roses from that giant chip he's got on his shoulder. I'm patient, though. I can wait him out. Hopefully, he might tell me the truth before I kick him out of here.

"It's a bit late for lunch but too early for dinner," I muse. "I could put together a snack now, though, and make something substantial later." I don't admit it out loud, but I've got that whiskey sloshing around my stomach, and I wouldn't mind some carbs to soak it up. Yes, a bite or two to eat sounds very sensible indeed.

"Why are you being nice?" he blurts out, causing me to turn around. His face has gone all red again, and he's waving his hands around fretfully despite his recent cut. "You're not what I expected you to be."

I arch an eyebrow. Ah. So he had expectations of me? That's interesting.

"We might have an unusual arrangement, Jack," I say patiently as I open my fridge. "But you are still a guest in my home. I suggested this solution, so now it's my responsibility to look after you whilst you're here. If that's okay with you?"

I glance over and see him squirm on his stool. Hmm. He's not used to being looked after, is he?

I have to be brutally honest with myself and admit that I wouldn't be offering this arrangement to just anyone. If he were some ugly, obnoxious wanker, I'd have just called the police like any sane person would have done. But there's something about this pretty but prickly young man that's calling to me. He's broken, and lord help me, but I want to try and fix it, even if it's only in a small way.

"Fine," he mumbles in response to my question. "But we're not mates. I don't like you, and I'm only here because you were crazy enough not to call the police. I'll work off my debt, then I'll be gone. Is *that* okay?"

"Yes, Jack," I say, hiding my face behind the fridge door so he doesn't see my amusement.

He's still fighting me, and I can't help but relish that. He's not going to open up right away or even at all. But I take it as a small victory that he lets me feed him some pita bread and veggies that we dip in hummus. Once he's made a dent in that, I quietly put out some olives and salami slices as well as pouring him some lemonade. We don't talk, but the more food he consumes, the more relaxed I see his shoulders become.

He's my project, I realise. He's going to work for me, yes, but in turn I'm going to fuss over him. It's been so long since I had anyone in my life like that. And this is safe because it has an expiry date. I can treat him like a trial run for getting off my arse and back into the real world. I've hidden away in this tower for far too long now.

He can remind me how to be human again, and I can show him a little pampering, even if it is somewhat forced upon him.

I'm fully aware of how fucked up this all is, but to be blunt, what's the point of having obscene amounts of money if you can't act on a mad whim from time to time? No one's getting hurt—quite the opposite, in fact. So I'm going to play the eccentric card and have a little fun.

And who knows? After a couple of days, maybe Jack won't hate me anymore.

Or at least, maybe he'll hate me just a little bit less.

CHAPTER 6

Jack

I wake from a deep sleep completely disorientated, and panic grips my chest. *Where am I? What's going on?* But then I blink and take in my surroundings, steadying my breathing as my memories slowly come back to me.

I'm in Felix's guest bedroom—or more likely *one* of his guest bedrooms. He hasn't exactly given me a tour of the penthouse, but it's definitely got a lot more rooms than I've seen so far.

And yet it's just him rattling around in this big old place.

I shake my head and rub sleep from my eyes. I must still be groggy if I'm feeling sorry for the lonely, evil billionaire.

Except I sigh and stare out of the window, marvelling at all the trailing plants hanging from what I assume to be an outdoor balcony above. We're so high up it seems crazy to see anything through the glass aside from open air and low-hanging clouds. Even birds seem scarce from what I can tell.

I reclaim my train of thought. I sighed because after an evening spent in his company, Felix doesn't seem evil at all. The mere fact that I'm even calling him Felix says it all. He's…kind of goofy. A fact that my brain doesn't want to fully compute, but it's true. And he hasn't just given me an alternative to prison. He's genuinely being kind.

I don't get it.

After he patched me up and fed me, he was true to his word and found me some tough gardening gloves so I could continue to try and safely fish out all of the antique coins from the mess of glass. He gave me pictures detailing the entire collection, and I'm starting to appreciate what a pain in the arse it's going to be putting it all back together.

However, he only let me work for maybe a couple of hours before he called me out again. I could feel he was keeping an eye on me. My skin was prickling the whole time from feeling his eyes on me, and I have to be brutally honest and admit that it wasn't a wholly unpleasant experience.

But I knew he was puttering about in the kitchen, and after a while, I could smell something delicious cooking. Sure enough, I emerged from my task to discover he'd made us steak with buttery mashed potatoes and an assortment of veggies. He seemed genuinely thrilled to be able to cook for someone else, and chatted aimlessly at me as we ate at the breakfast bar again, all very casual, and I have to admit, quite pleasant.

Which forces me to yet again ask the question: why doesn't this handsome, rich AF dude have any friends? He's certainly *friendly* enough. Like a ray of sunshine through my stormy clouds. I should find it hellishly annoying, but instead, I find that it's slowly chipping away at my defences against him.

This man is my enemy. He tried to hurt my mum. Why am I laughing at his corny jokes?

He showed me to the room I'm currently lying in at just gone nine. I was irritated to be given a bedtime by this stranger, especially one so early, but I must have passed out pretty much right away, as I don't remember staring at the walls at all. And glancing at the clock beside my bed tells me I've slept in till almost ten in the morning. That's wild.

I've never experienced such an amazing mattress or pillows, though. I can't say I've ever wasted money on getting a massage before, but after last night, I imagine this is what I'd feel like after having one. It's as if all my muscles have been kneaded and cradled.

The decor in here is lacking in personality like the rest of the place I've seen so far. All except the vault. I was right in thinking that's where he hides away who he truly is. But who's he hiding *from?* It's clear he's starved of company, so I doubt many people are coming up here to visit him.

I huff angrily and slap my hands on top of the duvet. I don't *care* what his story is or why such a seemingly kind and generous person is up here all alone. I came here to settle a score. To get a payday. Fuck, if he's that wealthy and charitable, I'll just *ask* him for money at the end of it.

Something cold slithers through me. No, I won't be doing that. That seems…sordid. Icky.

And robbing him will be so much better?

I squirm in the bed and try not to think too hard about how much easier that will be because I won't have to look him in the eye to do it.

No. I can't catch feelings or let my guard down. Just because he's being a bit nice doesn't negate what he did or the fact that *I'm his prisoner.* A very cushy prisoner, granted. But a prisoner, nonetheless.

Because I broke into his home and tried to steal from him.

Urgh, this whole situation is so fucked up. He might not be a saint, but I'm definitely not one, either. I guess we're both a little morally grey. The important difference being that he's literally a billionaire and I'm in this mess because I didn't want to see my mother get turfed out onto the streets in winter.

My belly rumbles, and I need to pee. At least I have an en suite, so I can relieve myself without having to venture out of the room, but without a change of clothes, I actually don't want to shower. The thought of putting sweaty, slept-in underwear back on makes me gag. I could go commando, but that idea makes me feel oddly exposed in this stranger's home.

And then there's the issue of food. I hate that I have to rely on him and can't just feed myself. I'm used to going hungry. That's not really the issue. It's knowing there's a shit ton of supplies down in that fancy, shiny kitchen, and I feel like I can't touch any of it. It makes me resentful and seems like a pretty good metaphor for the whole rich and poor dynamic in society at large.

I don't want to be at the mercy of his handouts. I want to take care of myself. I don't need anyone else.

To my horror, I realise my eyes have become itchy with hot tears. Okay…maybe it's not that I don't *want* anyone to take care of me. It's that I know it won't happen. Just because he was a bit nice to me yesterday doesn't mean I can get used to it. He's not going to dote on me today. Chances are he's already become bored of the gimmick of having me around to fix up his coin collection display. He's probably already more than eager to get me out of his home.

I angrily grab my backpack so I can fish out my pill packet and take one with the glass of water that he provided. Then I wash up in the bathroom and run my fingers through my hair. He left me a whole bunch of skincare products and the like, but I'm feeling bitter now and don't want his charity. I do give in and brush my teeth as a matter of pride, though. I don't want to have morning breath around him for whatever reason.

It's embarrassing how long it takes to psych myself up to open my door and venture out into the hallway. No other soul ever needs to know, but I still cringe at myself. This guy is my *enemy*. I shouldn't be worried about feeling awkward in his home.

But I do.

Eventually, I just grab the door handle and dash out into the hall. Nothing terrible happens, so I edge over to the lip of the interior balcony and look down on top of the kitchen and living room area.

And frown.

There's a lot of food laid out on the breakfast bar, and I mean a lot. There's also a load of shopping bags clustered on one of the coffee tables. Is he having a party? Doing a magazine shoot? I honestly can't wrap my head around it.

But my stomach rumbles loudly, and I realise how hungry I am despite the good dinner he fed me last night. I guess I have been surviving a lot lately on tinned soup and packets of instant noodles. Getting some actual fruit and veg into my system was a bit of a shock, I'm sure.

I lose the battle with my pride and trot down the stairs, following my nose towards the smells of sizzling bacon and brewing coffee.

I should have appreciated that Felix would probably be around. It's not like trained mice would have got all this together. But I pull up short as I rush onto the lower level and see him there in the kitchen. He's got loose-fitting chinos on and another crisp white shirt that's straining over his bulging form. He's not ripped like a body builder, but he's certainly large and I don't hate that the shirt leaves little to the imagination.

But what really fries my brain is that he's got music playing quietly from somewhere, and he's bopping from side to side as he tends to the bacon cooking on the hob. It's so…*cute*. How is that possible?

I don't get long to dwell on it, because a voice shrieks from overhead, and I can safely say it's *not* Felix who's speaking.

"Good morning!" The pitchy, nasally words fill the mostly quiet penthouse, and I immediately duck for cover, my heart leaping into my throat. Felix spins around in concern, then laughs.

"Goose!" he cries in delight, holding out his arm. I peek through my fingers and see a huge green bird swoop above me, diving down to land on Felix's elbow. The bird has a sharp-looking orangey-yellow beak and flashes of blue and red under their wings as well as through their tail.

"Goose?" I repeat faintly. "That's a parrot."

Felix scrunches up his nose and bumps it against the bird's neck. "An eclectus parrot, to be precise," he says proudly. "This is my golden boy. Isn't that right, Goose?"

"Good morning! Tickety-boo! Hello, hello, Felix, hello! Row, row, row your boat!"

I open and close my mouth as I slowly rise back up to my full height. Realising there isn't actually a threat doesn't stop my heart from pounding in my chest, but I try and take a few subtle deep breaths before my captor notices how freaked out I was.

"He's not used to visitors or a change in routine," Felix goes on to explain like nothing is wrong. "So he was hiding all yesterday evening. But I'm glad he's come out of hiding now. Say hello to our new friend Jack, Goose!"

The bright green bird bobs his head several times, saying, "Hello hello hello!" I can't help but smile. I've never seen a talking bird before, and Goose is funny the way he jerks about and squawks. I flinch as he suddenly flaps his wings, though, and jumps up to perch on Felix's head.

"Naughty boy," Felix says, sounding anything but annoyed. "He's just showing off. Don't mind him. Did you sleep well? If you're hungry, I've made breakfast."

"For how many people?" I ask faintly, stepping closer to the spread he's laid out. I see fresh pastries and fruit, different types of cereal and several kinds of milk, cold meats and cheese, a butter tray, and half a dozen flavours of jam, as well as peanut butter, honey, and marmalade. That's not even including the hot scrambled eggs, hash browns, a bowl of baked beans, and fried mushrooms and tomatoes.

"Oh, don't worry about that," he says with a shrug. "Anything that won't keep, I'll box up and send over to the halfway house I support around the corner."

"Halfway house?" I repeat. "Is that like a homeless shelter?"

He wobbles his head from left to right. "It's temporary housing for LGBTQIA runaways. Just a place they can rest and get back on their feet if they've had to leave home in a hurry."

My stomach drops out from under me, and suddenly, I don't feel so hungry anymore. "Queer teens?" I whisper.

He nods, going back to the bacon that he flips over. "Over fifty percent of homeless teenagers identify as not cishet," he says matter-of-factly. "Did you know that? I make sure the house—well, it's more like a hotel, I guess—has proper furniture, bedding, computers, other home and kitchen wear, that sort of thing. If those kids are still studying, they can't exactly work too much and earn enough to rent somewhere. The house gives them a grace period to save up, feel safe, then head out into the world again."

There's a lump in my throat, and I don't know what to say, so I just sit down at the breakfast bar, looking incredulously at the wealth of food before me.

How is this the same man who callously made my mum

and hundreds of others redundant? He might not realise it, but he's effectively threatened her with homelessness. Yet he's conscious enough to already have a plan to box up his leftovers from this lavish feast and make sure it goes somewhere where who knows how many people might appreciate it.

I'm so fucking confused.

"Jack?" Felix says, pulling me from my reverie. I blink and look up to see his concerned face. Goose is bouncing on his shoulder now, chattering to himself and…is he *singing?* Not just quoting song lyrics. There's almost a tune to that old Queen song he's muttering.

"Uh," I say, collecting myself. "Yeah, fine. Just waking up still. That's very nice of you to help those kids out. Did you make all this for me?"

"Well, and me," he says with a wink. "Goose will have some, too. His diet is mostly parrot pellets, but he needs veggies as well. That's why there's sweet potato and carrots and the like." He points to a dish of more savoury items that I hadn't noticed.

I nod faintly, feeling overwhelmed. "Thank you," I whisper. "But you really didn't need to. This is…a lot."

Felix grins as he slides the crispy bacon rashers onto a plate that he adds to the collection. "I didn't know what you'd like. Besides, like I said, I know it won't go to waste. Teenagers are like bottomless pits when it comes to food." He laughs heartily, those beautiful crinkles appearing around his eyes again.

Something breaks inside me. He *is* beautiful, isn't he? But none of this is adding up with what I know to be facts. I feel sick.

"Dig in," he says with a nod as he grabs a pitcher of fresh orange juice. "Did you want some of this? Or I've got tea or coffee."

I shake my head and swallow, not trusting myself to speak. I'm surprised that he doesn't push. He just leaves the jug on the table and starts helping himself quietly to a selection of different kind of foods.

After a few minutes, I stop freaking out and manage to unknot my stomach enough to pick up a croissant and start nibbling. It's so light and crisp that my hunger comes back, so I pause long enough to find a knife and spread butter and raspberry jam on the flat side of it. I feel Felix watching me as I eat, but I ignore him for now. My emotions are all over the place, and I need a few more minutes to collect myself.

Luckily, Goose is here to provide a running commentary of random words. He says a lot of "good boy" and "thank you" and "pretty boy, Goose, pretty, pretty boy". Right now he's singing more 'Row, row, row your boat' despite the fact that Felix's chilled pop music playlist is still running. I can't help but kind of like the cacophony as it's all reasonably quiet. The discord should be aggravating, but instead, I find that it's soothing something in me.

"Thank you," I manage to say again, meaning it more sincerely this time. "I like that you aren't just going to throw everything away. A lot of people in your position would."

He gives me a crooked smile that makes my stomach flip again. The croissant stays down, thankfully. "I have a compost bin on the roof for most of my food waste," he says. "But a proper spread like this…yeah, I'd never let it go to waste."

I nod, believing him. I think it's getting to the point where I'm going to have to confront him because this isn't making sense. He needs to explain his completely contradictory behaviour if we're going to be spending the next few days together.

Speaking of which…

"Um," I say, trying not to get awkward. But needs must.

"Do you think I could maybe use a washing machine at some point?"

He blinks, probably confused by my non sequitur. "Uh, yeah, sure. Why?"

I lick my lips and try not to blush. I feel like I've had nothing but flaming cheeks since I got here. "I don't have any spare clothes," I say as delicately as I can. Unless he wants me to start smelling, I'll probably need to do something about that sooner rather than later.

"Oh," he says brightly, and Goose starts dancing again on his shoulder with a loud squawk. "Of course. I've already taken care of that. I was just going to wait until after breakfast. All that over there is for you."

I frown, looking over my shoulder. I freeze as I realise he's indicating the coffee table.

The coffee table covered in various shopping bags. *Clothing* shopping bags, now I'm actually paying attention.

I turn back and look in disbelief at Felix. This man, my captor.

He went clothes shopping for me?

No. He probably got someone to go clothes shopping *for* him for me.

I don't know if that makes it better or worse. My head is swimming, and the croissant churns in my stomach. I shake my head, feeling dizzy.

"But…*why?*" I finally manage to blurt out.

CHAPTER 7
Felix

Jack looks like his brain is short-circuiting. For a second, I almost feel bashful, but I made myself behave and didn't let my assistant go too overboard. Besides, the money I spent on those clothes I probably earned in under ten minutes today already. Probably only a minute, thinking about it. What doesn't fit or he doesn't like, I'll just give to the halfway house. It won't go to waste.

I shrug and flash him a grin. "I could hardly offer you any of my clothes to lend. In case you hadn't noticed, I'm a fucking unit."

I'm disappointed when he doesn't laugh. He's still staring at me, shaking his head faintly. "I tried to rob you. I broke into your home. I get we made an arrangement, but I don't get why you're buying me *gifts*."

"It's just a practicality," I say, and I mean it. "I can't expect you to suffer in the same clothes for however long you're here."

"But you bought me half of Oxford Street!"

I chuckle. "Now that's a bit of an exaggeration. It looks

like a lot because everything is duplicated in two or three sizes. I wasn't sure of your measurements, you see."

He continues to gawk at me for another few moments until I start to wonder if I really did cross a line. I'm sure I haven't, but he just looks so…outraged.

"Eighteen years," he says eventually.

I feel my eyebrows raise. "Come again?"

"Eighteen years my mum worked for your company," he says flatly, his eyes boring into mine. "Rarely called in sick, had to be bullied into taking all her holiday allowance. She even organised the charity raffle at the Christmas party every year for the last decade. Then *bam*. You close her branch and make everyone redundant without severance packages the month before Christmas. She's approaching sixty, living paycheque to paycheque, and thanks to you, she won't be able to make next month's rent. She's going to be out on the street. So tell me, Mr Generosity, just *how* do you justify *that?*"

He's yelling by the time he stops talking. His fists are balled, and his face has gone all red and blotchy again. Except this time, it doesn't seem so adorable.

Horror is blossoming in my gut. "*I* did that?" I ask faintly.

"She was told the order came from up high, from the big boss, and there was nothing that could be done. That's you, isn't it?"

I realise Goose has gone quiet, and he nibbles my ear as if he's asking the same question. I feel sick. Not just because of the accusation he's levelling at me but because I have no idea what he's talking about. I'm so detached from this company that I never wanted to inherit, but did I really fire all those people like he's claiming without even remembering that I did it?

How heartless have I become?

"What branch?" I ask as I retrieve my phone from my

pocket. There has to be an answer somewhere in my emails or files.

He crosses his arms over his small chest, his eyes shiny with unshed tears. My heart cracks. I might not know this young man well—or at all, in fact. But I'm already rather fond of him and I hate that I've caused him and his family so much pain.

"Dagenham," he bites out.

"Oh," I say, immediately understanding what's happened. Or at least having a very good guess, which I confirm with a quick internet search. "My shareholders convinced me to sell that branch as well as half a dozen others this summer. The new company must have liquidated the assets for profit."

Jack's eyes go wide, but I can't say that I feel much better. I never gave a second thought to the human beings who worked on those sites. My CFO just presented me with numbers, and I signed off on whatever would make the bigwigs on the board happy. They're the ones with proper business degrees and decades of experience. I'm just the fool whose grandfather happened to build the company from the ground up.

"But I checked it was you," Jack splutters. "On the internet. It didn't say anything about a sale."

"I'm sure they kept it all very hush-hush to stop people from protesting too much," I say glumly.

"Hush-hush," Goose repeats.

Wanting to show him some sort of proof, I pull up a PDF of the contract. "Obviously, I don't expect you to read all of that," I say. "But if you glance at the first few paragraphs, then scroll to the end, you'll find my signature. Jack, I'm so sorry. I really had no idea."

Jack covers his mouth with his hand, looking mortified. I'm sure it's nothing compared to how I'm feeling. "So it wasn't even you," he says.

I shrug dejectedly and put my phone away. "It might as well have been. Negligence and malice might be different intentions, but if they end up in the same results, does it really matter? Am I to assume this is why you chose to break into my house and rob me?"

Jack drops his hand. He's a petite man anyway, but he looks so small in that moment. "Yes," he says simply. "I had to look after my mum. I wanted to make you pay."

I exhale, puffing out my cheeks. "Right. Yeah, well, that's fair enough. Extreme, but it makes sense."

"No, it doesn't make sense at all," Jack says angrily. He tugs at his hair and throws himself back down in the seat opposite me again. "It was an insane plan fuelled by rage and fear. I should have just tried to help her get a new job or asked her wanker of a landlord if he'd pause her rent until the new year or something."

I hesitate for a second, but then I throw caution to the wind and reach out to cover his small hand with my large one. "I think it was actually quite remarkable. Not to mention brave."

He narrows his eyes at me, but he doesn't pull his hand away, and my heart does a little victory dance. "You think it was remarkably brave of me to commit several crimes."

I grin, the heaviness lifting from my heart. "Yeah," I tell him honestly.

Because I can fix this. I can certainly see to it that Jack's mother doesn't have to worry about her next few months' rent, and possibly even get her a new job elsewhere in the company. This also might be the kick up the arse I need to stop coasting and actually take a more active role in my family's legacy. My grandfather would be so disappointed in me if he were still alive, but I can salvage the situation. I shouldn't be letting people down like that.

"No harm done," I say.

"Tell that to your coin collection," he quips with an eyeroll, and I laugh.

"Nothing that can't be fixed," I assure him, especially as he's the one who's going to be doing the fixing. "But the fact that you were willing to go to such lengths and put yourself at such personal risk says a lot about your character, Jack."

"Yeah, it says that I'm an idiot," he says, but he shoots me a little mischievous smirk. It feels like an olive branch, moving us tentatively towards something more like friendship.

It's embarrassing how much I want Jack to be my friend. He's like no one else in my life with his hot-headedness and tattoos, not to mention that his youth makes him feel like a breath of fresh air. I swear I'm surrounded by dusty old men all the time these days, even if it's only via video conferences.

"The clothes are yours," I say gently, jutting my chin in the direction of all the shopping bags. "Why don't you go and have a shower, and I'll bring everything up to your room for you to try on. That is, if you've had enough breakfast." It's not escaped my attention that he only had a single croissant. I know he's small, but he's got to need more than that to keep him going.

He sighs and nods. "Actually, I could eat a little more. If that's okay with you?"

I indicate the multitude of food still left before us. "That's literally what I made it for. Please fill your boots." To encourage him, I help myself to more eggs and bacon, putting the plate in the microwave to heat it up a little again. "You want some too?" I ask, sensing the way he's watching me.

"Um…yes, please," he says shyly.

It pleases me greatly to see him pile up his own plate for me to blast. He also nibbles on some grapes and cheese. I appreciate that I've always liked feeding people, especially lovers. It makes me feel as if I'm taking care of them properly.

Not that Jack is a lover, obviously. But my hope that he could become a friend is growing.

"I'm really sorry," he says after a while, placing his fork down and wiping his mouth. He catches my gaze, his green eyes full of remorse. "I wanted to make you pay, and it wasn't even your fault."

We've already gone over how it is still partially my fault, but rehashing that isn't what Jack needs right now.

He needs absolution.

"I accept your apology," I tell him. "But I'm not sorry."

He frowns at me. "I trashed all your precious things," he says uncertainly.

I offer him a crooked grin. "Nothing's actually broken beyond repair, though. And if you hadn't snuck into my home, we never would have met."

That pretty blush blooms on his cheeks again, and this time, I get to enjoy it.

"You're so weird," he says with a laugh. "Most people don't try and befriend their burglars."

I smile fully at that. "I'm not most people," I inform him proudly.

"You're not, are you?" he murmurs. "I'm...I'm glad."

"That I'm a stereotypical eccentric billionaire?" I quip, but he shakes his head.

"I'm glad that you're not actually a villain," he says, a softness in his eyes as he looks at me. "It means I'm allowed to like you. Especially if you insist on buying me ridiculous presents."

I wag my finger at him. "Not ridiculous, practical," I remind him. But secretly my heart is dancing in my chest again.

He likes me.

I don't care if I'm acting like a fourteen-year-old with a crush. I want him to like me. I want him to enjoy the time he spends here.

I want him to want to be here. Not be here because I've made him.

"Speaking of which, do you want to go try your clothes on now?" I ask.

He laughs again. Every time it's lighter and more carefree. I'm starting to crave it.

"I swear you're more excited than I am," he says, shaking his head. His words aren't unkind, though. Just gently teasing.

"I am," I say. "I gave my PA instructions, but I'm not sure what she and the team were able to get on such short notice."

"You had a whole team storm the shops for me?" he asks, his voice sweet and quiet. Oh, god help me. I just want to spoil the shit out of him if it means he'll look at me like that with those pretty eyes.

"I wanted to make sure everything was here before you woke up," I say like it was just a practical decision on my part.

I know full well I could have asked my PA for just a pair of jeans, a T-shirt, and a pack of underwear. Jack didn't need a whole new wardrobe. But the bossy bastard in me wanted the thrill of seeing him in the clothes I bought him.

I want to mark him, like an animal.

If I can't get my hands on him, I'll take the next best option.

But maybe I don't have to. Because this time, it's him who reaches out and places his hand over mine, giving it a little squeeze. "Thank you," he says. "I mean it. You really are incredibly kind, Felix. I'm sorry I ever thought otherwise."

I flip my hand so we're palm to palm, squeezing it right

back. "My pleasure, Jack. Now go on and shower. I'll deliver your clothes, and then I'll expect a fashion show."

"I'll polish up my strut," he says, and it feels like flirtation the way he bats his eyelashes at me.

My grumpy little thief has some playfulness in him after all. I wonder what else he's got lurking beneath the surface.

I can't wait to find out.

CHAPTER 8

Jack

I'M NOT ENTIRELY SURE HOW I'M FEELING, BUT I'M DEFINITELY feeling a certain kind of way.

Felix was true to his word and ferried up every single bag into 'my' room whilst I was taking a shower. But then he also produced an armchair from somewhere and has been sitting out in the corridor, waiting patiently for me to come out and show him each of my ensembles in turn.

And there have been quite a few.

Once I found a pair of jeans that fitted perfectly, there were then several T-shirts, Henleys, shirts, and jumpers that went with them. I appreciate that Felix's team got me a few sizes to try and that one from each of them was bang on. I also feel a bit emotional that because of their forward-thinking, someone (or many someones, most likely) at the LGBT charity is going to get new clothes as well.

I'm so glad I finally confronted Felix about what I thought he'd done. It all makes so much more sense now that ultimately, he had nothing to do with my mum losing her job. It sounds like he might be pretty checked out of his job, which isn't a great thing either when stuff like this can happen as a consequence. But he seemed genuinely contrite and keen to make amends.

I hated seeing him upset. I'm the thundercloud. It's better when he's the ray of sunshine. That way, we balance each other out.

It's crazy to think that this time yesterday we hadn't even met. I was a bundle of nerves getting ready for this job. Now, I'm not sure what I'm doing. Other than trying on a really beautiful pair of black trousers with a subtle snakeskin print embossed on the material. They aren't something I'd even think to try on (and not just because I caught a glimpse of the price tag, yikes), but because Felix has given them to me, I feel like I can be daring. I pair them with a purple shirt and a pair of pointy, shiny shoes. I guess he checked the size on the pair of boots that I took off and left by the door, because there's only one option of those, and they fit perfectly.

I roll the sleeves of the shirt up, not attempting to hide my tattoos. Felix is more than aware of who I am by now, and I don't feel like I have to try and hide so I can fit in with his posh lifestyle.

The only thing that would make this outfit even better would be to finish it off with my dad's leather jacket. I feel a pang in my chest but try to rub it away. Micky's keeping it safe for me, and I'll get it back, one way or another. Then I can put it on top of these amazing new clothes.

If Felix lets me keep them. If he just wants me to wear them here, that's okay. I'll understand. I feel like there's a...*thing* going on here. Like a power dynamic. I'm pretty sure he's getting off on dressing me and feeding me and all that. Like I said before, I'm at his mercy, but instead of being oppressive, it's kind of...sexy.

I'm not sure. I've never really had a decent relationship

before. There have been guys I've fucked regularly for lengths of time and friends with benefits. But I don't know what it's like to actually date anyone, let alone what it would be like to have someone want to be that kind of controlling. I'd always assumed it was a red flag type of behaviour. But with Felix, it doesn't feel mean or suffocating. It feels like he cares.

I give myself a light slap on the face and laugh. We're in a strange situation, for sure. But we're not *dating*. We only just met, and if I'm being brutally honest, there's still a chance he could call the police on me.

In my heart, though, I do think that's very unlikely now.

"I'm not sure why you thought I'd need fancy threads like this to sweep up glass," I say as I step out of my room and give him a twirl. "But I love it all. Thank you."

I grin and stop spinning to look at him, but he doesn't say anything. His mouth is hanging open, and his eyes are wide. After a second, he clears his throat and shakes his head. "Very nice," he grunts.

"Very nice!" Goose squawks, bobbing up and down on Felix's shoulder. "Pretty boy, pretty boy, pretty boy."

"You're right, Goose. He is," Felix says with a wink, apparently having recovered himself. My cheeks flame, and yet again, I wonder if my jolly giant is just having fun or if he's really flirting.

Now I know he's not the ogre I thought he was, I kind of want it to be flirting.

"Well," I say sadly. "That's the last of it. I'll separate the stuff I'm keeping from the rest you're going to send to the halfway house and get changed into something a little more practical. Thank you again, Felix. I really do appreciate it. It's extremely generous of you."

"My pleasure," he murmurs.

His gaze lingers on me, and I bustle back into my room before my mind can veer off into a thoroughly debauched direction. I'm tempted to jump back into the shower and make it a really cold one. But by the time I get changed and have been focused on sorting out all the clothes, I manage to calm myself down. I get a real kick out of hanging all my new things in Felix's otherwise previously empty wardrobe. I'm like a magpie. I can't stop staring at all my treasures.

Eventually, I emerge once again from my room with all the spare clothes bagged back up and equally divided between my hands. The armchair is gone, so I go to find my giant new friend.

I jog downstairs and leave the bags on the coffee table where I found them before. True to his word, Felix has boxed all the food up from breakfast and presumably had it collected to give to the halfway house.

It's crazy to me that he's got all these people at his beck and call, and I wonder once more why he's choosing to hide himself away up here in the clouds. He's clearly a social person. Why is he isolating himself like this?

Maybe I'll find out. I'm going to be here for at least a few days, I'm sure. And then...

Then what? I hadn't really thought about it until this very second. Are we really going to stay in touch? The billionaire CEO and the lowly thief? It seems highly unlikely. And I don't know what's wrong with me, but the thought makes me sad. God, I haven't even known this guy for twenty-four hours, and he's not kicking me out for a while at least. There's nothing to mope about.

Yet.

"Get a grip," I mutter to myself and shake my whole body. I'm being ridiculous.

What I need to do is focus on my job. It doesn't feel like

I'm being forced into a task I resent anymore. I'm righting a wrong I accidentally did to a friend. We're friends now, right? There's a connection between us that's undeniable, that's for sure.

When I reach the open safe, I'm surprised to see Felix has set himself up outside it in the hall at a table and chair. He's wearing a pair of silver-framed glasses that highlight both his blue eyes and the grey in his thick, dark hair. I already knew he was handsome—you just have to have eyes to see that. But something about the glasses makes my heart flip.

God, he's gorgeous.

"Hey," I say softly and indicate where he's carefully sorting out his coins, already setting some of them back into their individual slots within the red velvet display. "You putting me out of a job?" As soon as the words leave my mouth, I wince and regret them. He looks up at me like he's not sure if I'm joking or not. "Sorry. That was in poor taste."

He might not have directly made my mum redundant, but his company is partly responsible. I don't want him to think I still blame him, though. He might have been a bit careless, but it was actually the new company that threw all the employees under the bus right before the holiday season.

"Don't be sorry," he says warmly. "I just figured that two pairs of hands are better than one. Besides, I know this collection extremely well, so it'll be much easier for me to do this part of it if you can keep finding the coins themselves amid the glass and then sweep that up."

I nod, already reaching for my protective gloves. He's also wearing a pair, but they're the same latex kind that he used when he patched up my cut yesterday. I put a fresh plaster on after my shower, and it's already looking much better.

I love that Felix did that for me. I felt so safe under his care. Not enough to want to get hurt again, but enough to daydream about other ways he could take care of me whilst I sift through the glass some more, slowly sweeping the debris into a sturdy bin once I'm sure no coins are still mixed in with it.

I have to be careful not to daydream too vividly. Otherwise, I'm going to end up with a situation in my brand-new jeans.

"Why did you start collecting coins?" I ask, genuinely curious to know.

He pauses from his work out in the corridor and looks up in consideration for a minute before giving me his attention. "My grandfather gifted me my first one, and I think it was intended to be exactly as pretentious as it appears."

"Oh, it's not…" I begin, but the lie dies on my tongue. I thought he was an absolute wanker when I realised he was so rich he even collected money. It would be embarrassing for us both if I were to pretend otherwise. "Yeah, it's pretty pretentious," I admit with a laugh that he joins in on.

"Yeah," he says with a sigh. "Granddad placed a hell of a lot of stock in reputation. He liked to flash things around that let other people know just how well he'd done for himself. All I'd wanted that Christmas was a Game Boy. But he gifted me a Roman coin instead that he'd procured from a private collector, letting me know just how much it had cost him to do so. At the time, I didn't give a shit. But as the years went on and he got me a few more, I became fascinated with the idea. I look at every single one of these coins and wonder who held them in their long existences. What joy did they bring? What luxuries or essentials did they bring their brief owners before they were passed on and on and on?"

I look down at the Spanish peseta that I've just plucked from the sea of glass. "That's actually incredibly beautiful," I admit. "Romantic, even. I'd never thought of such a thing.

But I guess you could look at all money like that. Lots of objects, actually."

He hums, and I look up to see him beaming at me. "I think so," he says warmly. "Money to me isn't about greed. It's about freedom. Opportunity. Hope. I look at this vast collection of mine, and it's like I can feel the energy through the years of what these little bits of metal gave to people."

"Wow," I say, turning the peseta over in my fingers.

"Of course, I am fully aware of how selfish it is to hoard a collection like this," he says with a rueful chuckle. "It should be in a museum."

I frown and look around at the various items in his safe. "As long as you haven't stolen anything, surely it's your stuff to do with as you see fit?"

He tilts his head and raises his eyebrows like I've made a fair point. "Perhaps. It's in my will that it will go to a suitable home once I'm gone, though. It feels like something that should be appreciated by as many people as possible."

I shrug. "Nothing wrong with you getting to enjoy it in the meantime, though."

"And now you can, too," he says with such tenderness that it makes my eyes snap up to look at him again.

"Yeah," I say softly. Guilt slices through me, thinking about how I was still planning on pinching something from here as recently as this morning. But I think about the joy in his eyes as he talks about the history that comes with everything in here, and I can't. I just can't.

Even if that means I'll have to lose the only connection I had left with my dad. But fair's fair. If Micky wants to hold the jacket hostage until I can pay him, that's what I'll have to accept. Even if that day never comes.

I'm not ripping off Felix now. He wasn't the one who hurt my mum. He's a good person who doesn't deserve to be taken advantage of.

I'll manage somehow. And if he'll let me keep them, I'll be managing in the nicest clothes I've ever owned. That's something at least.

It might just have to be enough. Because I'm not betraying Felix Fagiolo now.

He's my friend. Even if it's just for a few days.

CHAPTER 9

Jack

The next few days pass in a bit of a blur. I should be bored. I should be itching to get my phone back, make a dash from this place, and return to my normal life.

But I'm not.

I don't want Mum to be worrying about me, obviously, and I don't want Micky doing anything stupid whilst I'm on radio silence. But I can't remember a time when I felt so calm and content. When all I had to worry about was what nice new clothes to wear. Felix insists on providing all my meals, most of which he cooks himself, and my little repair project is actually coming along quite well.

Is this what people do on holiday? I've never gone anywhere to lie on a beach or sip cocktails by a pool. It always seemed like such a shocking waste of money to me. But it's like my brain is being rinsed out with warm water. My back and neck are going to hate me when I eventually go back to my crappy bed and pillows.

I will have to leave at some point. I've only got a few more days' worth of meds for one thing. But also, the logical part of me knows that this is a weird fantasy bubble we've got ourselves in. It's not real life. He's a fucking *billionaire*. And I'm a petty thief who's done time. We might be having fun, but deep down I know I'm just a project for him. Like the coin display is for me. A social experiment.

That's okay, though, right? That's how holidays are supposed to work. You enjoy them for a couple of days or weeks, then you go home, refreshed.

I try to think of this as a new lease on life for me. A chance to start again. Not about how never seeing Felix again is more than likely going to break my heart more than just a little bit.

I love his happy smiles and easy laughs. I love the way he sings and dances to himself. I love his generosity. I even love his zany bird, named after a different kind of bird for a reason I still haven't quite worked out yet. There's still so much about him that's a mystery, and I lo…

I like him. Like. No other word beginning with 'l' because that would be insane.

I'm still not one hundred percent certain that he's gay. I'm very confident from a bunch of hints he's dropped, and I'm *sure* he's been flirting with me for days now. But without knowing beyond a doubt I don't want to get my hopes up about anything. I shouldn't hope, full stop. We're obviously completely incompatible from opposite sides of the tracks and have nothing in common.

So then why is his company so easy? Why does he warm my heart whenever we're together?

Not to mention what he does to other parts of his body. I might have had to…rectify…a couple of situations I've got myself into in the shower once or twice.

Or thrice.

"I've got an idea for those fancy clothes I bought you."

I blink and look up from where I've been working on finding a particular coin its home back on the display. All the glass is gone now, and Felix has ordered a new pane. He's also fixed the broken legs on the display case. I'm just trying to match up all the small coins with their correct-sized indents now. It's like working on a jigsaw puzzle and I'm finding it quite soothing.

I'm also losing track of time. I glance at the clock he's set up in here, as I don't have my phone to keep an eye on. It's almost six o'clock.

Felix is leaning against the doorframe of the safe, looking at me excitedly. He's been gone for the past few hours, doing I'm not sure what. I assumed maybe some actual work for his company, given how much time he's been spending with me these past couple of days.

"The fancy clothes?" I repeat.

He nods, and I finally notice that he's already put a nice pair of trousers on with a blue silk shirt. A couple of the buttons are undone, showing off a glimpse of dark hair on his chest. I try not to think too hard about licking it.

"Why don't you go put them on?" Felix suggests.

It's ridiculous, but my heart skips in my chest, and butterflies unfurl in my stomach. Nice clothes usually mean doing something nice. I try not to get my hopes up, but it's almost impossible with Felix grinning at me like an adorable puppy, practically dancing on the balls of his feet.

"Have I got time for a quick shower?" I ask, those nerves growing inside me. I'm not sure what's happening, but something is telling me that I should perhaps seize the opportunity to clean up if I can.

"Absolutely," Felix tells me warmly. "Come and meet me on the terrace once you're done."

I raise my eyebrows in surprise but also nod before watching him walk away. I've not been up there yet, but I know it's a sort of open-air space. That's where the trailing plants I can see out the window are hanging from.

Rather than trying to guess what's going on, I finish up with my work, making sure nothing has been left lying around that could get lost. I'm determined to put all these coins back exactly where they came from. Then I jog up to my room, strip off, and throw myself in the shower. I quickly rinse my hair and body with some all-in-one product, but then I take a little extra time to thoroughly freshen up my more intimate areas.

I'm being utterly foolish and am probably going to feel extremely embarrassed later, but I'd rather be over prepared than under. Besides, no one else need ever know, so the only person I have to worry about judging myself is me. And right now, I don't care if I'm being extra.

It's a long time since I've hoped for something like this.

Who could have possibly guessed that when I was planning this heist in a fit of rage that I'd end up swooning over the very guy I'd been intending to rob. Life is very strange sometimes.

I dry myself off and hastily put on underwear, the snake-skin trousers, and purple shirt, then spritz on the aftershave that mysteriously appeared in my bathroom yesterday. I didn't admonish Felix for giving me more gifts because I haven't been able to afford a scent for years, and selfishly, I don't want to have to give it back.

Whatever happens, this sweet and spicy fragrance will remind me of him and our time together until it runs out.

On a whim, I go digging in my backpack where I put my lucky penny for safe keeping, slipping it into my trouser pocket. I try not to analyse too closely what I might be hoping for luck *with*. I just know that I feel better having it on me for whatever's going to happen tonight.

I take one last glance in the mirror, happy with what I see.

I look cute. Sexy. I hope he can see that I've made an effort for him. I want to show him how grateful I am for all he's done for me over the past few days. Starting with not calling the police on me and then a hundred other caring things since.

The kaleidoscope of butterflies in my tummy takes flight as I exit my room, walk down the corridor, and begin jogging up to the top floor of the penthouse. Perhaps Felix just wants to show me the view and have a drink or something. That all sounds absolutely dreamy, if I'm honest.

But the reality is so much better.

I pause halfway through opening the door that leads onto the terrace, my jaw dropping open. My first thought is that it's not nearly as windy as I thought it would be, as there's safety glass that runs around the balcony almost all the way up to the ceiling. I can feel a breeze coming from above and in between the panes, but it's not a hurricane.

My second thought is that I can see a massive sectional sofa and a dining table with chairs, but it's almost hidden by the sheer volume of lush plant life. Countless pots cover the floor and other surfaces, not to mention the free-standing and wall trellises, making me feel like I've just stepped into a jungle of massive leaves and colourful flowers.

The third and most overwhelming thought is that there has to be a thousand white fairy lights twinkling at me. They have been entwined all over the trellises, around the pots, on the plants themselves, looped around the railing on the balcony, and hanging in streams against the interior walls. It's like some sort of enchanting wonderland.

And amidst it all stands Felix, two glasses of sparkling wine in his hands, apparently waiting for me. He's next to the table which I realised has been set for dinner. There are two covered plates, as well as bread, olives, salad, the bottle of

Champagne in a silver ice bucket, and even an honest to god candelabra, the flames dancing in the air current.

"Hi," he says, giving me a crooked smile. I swallow and close the door behind me, stepping out into the stunningly beautiful terrace.

"This is...did you do this?"

He laughs. "Which part? I grew the plants, yes. But I'll confess that's something I've been working on for years." He winks at me, and my tummy flips. I get close enough to take one of the Champagne flutes that he holds out. "I ordered the food, I'm afraid, but it's from one of my favourite places. Now, the fairy lights? That's what I've been working on all afternoon. They look pretty good, right?"

For a second, I don't trust myself to speak. I look around again until my throat is slightly less clamped. "It's beautiful," I say incredulously. "Did you...is this for me?"

Felix taps his glass to mine, making them chime like a bell. "You've been working hard. I wanted to take you out. There are places we could have gone. However, I don't mean to brag, but I don't think they'd have as good a view as this."

I shake my head in agreement. "It's lovely," I whisper. "Felix, I..."

Is this a date? What's happening here?

The words die in my mouth, though. Luckily, Felix isn't short of things to say. He raises his glass in a toast, beaming at me. "To an unlikely but exciting new friendship," he says.

He's certainly right about that.

"To us," I say before I can chicken out. But the way his eyes sparkle at me suggests that he quite likes my contribution.

We clink our glasses together again and, this time, also take a sip. This is the first time he's offered alcohol with a meal and I'm sure it's because he wanted to make sure we both had our heads on straight. Not saying I'm intending on getting smashed, but the fact that he's included it tonight indicates a somewhat more relaxed atmosphere.

"Check out the view," he says eagerly.

He places his hand on my lower back, and I have to bite my lip to stop myself from gasping in shock. God, his touch feels so good, even through my shirt. He gently steers me towards the glass, and I marvel at the breathtaking vista before us.

It's a clear evening, so we can see for miles even in the dark. The streetlights, car headlamps, and the lighting from inside businesses and people's homes glitter brightly. There's far too much light pollution from the city to be able to see much of the night sky, but it feels like all the artificial twinkling is more than making up for it.

"I feel like I'm swimming amongst the stars," I murmur. My voice is thick with emotion. Someone like me doesn't get to experience things like this. It's as if I'm in a dream, and I never want to wake up.

For a while, we just appreciate the city and sip our drinks. He keeps his hand on my back, and my heart dances in my chest the whole time. "Are you hungry?" he asks eventually. I nod and smile at him before he leads me back to the table and pulls out a chair for me to sit down. "This is the best lasagne in the whole of London, I swear."

He removes the silver cover from the plate in front of me, and the smell that wafts up is divine. My mouth waters immediately even though I had a good lunch mere hours ago. That becomes a distant memory as my stomach grumbles in anticipation of tasting what's on offer.

It's obviously been baked in the ceramic dish it's in, so it's still wonderfully hot as I cut into the layers of pasta, cheese, and meat sauce. I moan as I place the first bite on my tongue, not even feeling self-conscious as Felix watches me hungrily. The food is sublime.

So is my maybe-possibly-hopefully date.

Everything about this evening is perfect. It's like something out of a movie. I still can't quite believe it's happening.

And Felix did it all just for me.

I don't think I'm crazy. There's something building between us. And this feels like the night we find out exactly what.

CHAPTER 10
Felix

I know this is a date. We both know this is a date. I probably should have asked, but it feels more fun to have just told my little thief to look pretty and show up. I think we both prefer it that way.

Jack is gorgeous in the fancy ensemble I got my PA to buy him, even though I thought I was being ridiculous. At the time, I just got a kick out of imagining dressing him in something expensive, like he's a doll I own. But now I'm really glad I indulged myself because there's something inherently sexy about knowing I'm responsible for every inch of cotton and silk on his lithe body right now.

He sips his Champagne as he meets my gaze, giving a little chuckle. His cheeks have a rosy glow from the breeze and the alcohol and, I hope, a little bit from just pure pleasure.

"What?" he asks.

We finished eating a while ago and have just been enjoying the view and our drinks. There's a heater mounted on the wall above us, keeping us cosy, and more than enough illumination from all the fairy lights to see my date in the dark.

God, I want that more than anything.

For him to be mine.

It's entirely possible that I just haven't had a decent friendship in so many years that I'm latching on to the first bit of companionship that's come my way. But it doesn't feel like that. Jack lights up any room he's in. He might be prickly, but he's also fiery, and I'm drawn to his warmth like a moth to the flame.

I want to touch him like a famished man fantasises about a feast.

Jack raises his eyebrows, and I remember he asked me a question. "Just thinking about things," I say evasively.

"About me?" he asks, taking another sip of the drink that's obviously given him a little extra confidence.

I like to think I've made him comfortable as well. I'm not sure that life has been very kind to Jack Spriggs in the past. I know we're living in this crazy little bubble of ours right now, but I want to change that for him. I want to show him nothing but stability and luxury and kindness.

I also want to show him a *really* good time. I have no idea what's blossoming between us or if any kind of relationship would even be possible. But he's here now, and there's a tension growing that I've deliberately been encouraging all evening.

Hell, I've been attracted to him since the moment I laid eyes on the little fucker.

"I was just thinking how grateful I am to the universe that such a strange set of circumstances dropped you into my lap," I say, the honesty feeling hot and raw. But I'm not sure how much longer I can convince him to stay, and I don't want to waste any time that we could be using…better.

He blushes and shakes his head. "I don't think I'm ever going to get over the fact that I tried to rob you, and now we're…well, here."

He indicates the terrace, and every minute I laboured up here this afternoon to turn it into the most romantic setting I could was worth it. So was sneaking in the food and the embarrassing amount of time I spent manscaping in the bathroom. It's a long time since I entertained a friend. I can't even think of when I last had people up in my home for a social call.

I've missed it.

"I know," I agree. "But I'm glad. It's nice to host someone just for fun for a change instead of investors or board members or other people who bore me to tears."

I wink at him, but he glances at his Champagne flute, rubbing the stem thoughtfully before looking back up at me.

"Can I ask you a personal question, Felix?"

I shrug, trying to remain chilled. But it's difficult for me to stop my defences from immediately jumping up. It's been an age since I've done 'personal' with anyone, and whilst it might be what I want with him, it doesn't make it any less intimidating.

"Of course," I murmur.

He nods and licks his lips, apparently collecting his thoughts for a second. "You talk a lot about not having people over and being lonely. Contrary to my extremely screwed-up original opinion of you, you're actually a very nice person. You're generous and funny and, um, handsome." His blush deepens, but he soldiers on. "Why don't you have any friends? Or, um, a boyfriend?"

My heart aches. He's so cautious with his questions, clearly not wanting to hurt me. Which is such a victory in itself, considering what his objective was when he broke in here. But he's guessed correctly that it's a sensitive subject, and I can't fight the pang of grief and regret that surges through me.

"That's fair," I say, wanting him to know that he hasn't upset me or crossed a line. "I'd like to think I do have friends, but I absolutely keep them at arm's length." I frown and sigh. "I didn't use to be this bad. It's getting worse as I get older. I threw myself into the company for over fifteen years, but I don't even care about that anymore."

I realise I've been staring off into the middle distance when he covers my hand with his smaller one. I blink and turn my gaze to him, finding him smiling warmly. "I'm sorry," he says softly. "Is there a reason for that?"

I think about his dad and inhale slowly. If anyone could understand losing grip on reality due to bereavement, I'm sure it would be him. But it feels so stupid to me now. Other people moved on with their lives just fine. Pretty much everyone experiences loss. They don't cope with it by slowly descending into madness up in the clouds.

I rub my thumb against his hand, focusing on that. If I look him in the eye, I'm not sure I'll be able to get the words out.

"My first boyfriend was called Henry," I say, a sad smile playing on my lips. I can still see his face so perfectly in my mind. Rugged with sandy-blond hair and beard, green eyes that sparkled.

Green like Jack's. Huh.

I shake my head and focus on getting to the end of the story without totally ruining the mood of the evening. "We met in 1992 when I was seventeen and he was twenty-one. Back then, the age of consent for gay men was twenty-one, so we had to keep it secret. But we loved each other so much. I dreamed of spending the rest of my life with him. I know it was probably just puppy love, but he was gorgeous and selfless and made me feel like the centre of the whole universe."

I swallow around the lump in my throat and take another deep breath. Jack's hand is still in mine, giving me strength.

"I suppose you know a little of what it was like being gay in the eighties and nineties?" I ask him.

He tilts his head. "I was born in 1993," he admits, "but yeah."

My heart cracks a little. I don't know if I should read anything into it, but I can't help it. "Henry died in 1993," I manage to whisper.

There's a pause as he obviously thinks that through, putting two and two together. "From AIDS?" he asks, equally hushed. I nod, giving myself a moment before trying to speak again.

"We were always extremely careful, and he never passed it on to me. But I was with him until the very end. His family disowned him. We lost so many friends to it. And the media was out there doing their best to demonise us. I wasn't just devastated when he was gone. Even though I was closeted, I felt like I shouldn't be allowed near anyone in case it would taint them. And I was terrified of letting myself get close to anyone due to the danger of getting sick myself."

"Oh, Felix," Jack says thickly. I glance up and see his glassy eyes. Our grips tighten on each other's hands.

"It was a long time ago now," I say, not dismissing the levity of it, just stating facts. "To begin with, I became an island. I threw myself into work and my family's company, even though I never cared a jot about it. I kept my private life private and didn't date for years. Things gradually changed of course with all the medical advancements, and I tried to get out in the world again. Hook-ups were fine, but dating..." I scrub my hand over my face. "No matter how hard I tried, I just never knew how to let anybody in. And then I moved up here several years ago and just…stopped. I stopped trying to be a person and put a smile on to pretend I was all okay. I even let myself believe that was fine. Despite everything. I'm naturally quite a ridiculously positive person, in case you hadn't noticed."

I laugh, and he does too, but there are tears in both of our eyes.

"I might have noticed," he agrees.

"Then you crashed into my life," I whisper, "and without even realising what I was doing, I kept you hostage. You were like a whirlwind of life, and even though you thought you hated me, I could see a spark of something, and I couldn't let it go." I swallow and hold his gaze. "I'm sorry, Jack. I never should have coerced you to—"

"I'm HIV positive," he blurts out, the tears tumbling from his eyes.

I blink at him. "Huh?" I utter.

He crushes my hand in his. "I tested positive a few years ago. I'm so sorry that happened to your boyfriend. I can't lie about it now I know, though. I hope you don't hate me. I'm so sorry—"

"Hate you?" I say, my turn to interrupt. "Jack, I could never. Do you know how fucking happy that makes me? To know that you're healthy and alive and—oh *god!* Your medication?"

He's already shaking his head. "I had a sheet of pills with me. I thought for a second about claiming I didn't, thinking you might have to let me go. But…I didn't want to leave. Even with what I thought about you, I still couldn't help but be drawn to you. I'm glad I stayed, Felix. That we got a chance to get to know each other." He licks his lips and looks like he steels himself. "I don't want you to be lonely anymore. You don't have to hide or shelter people from you. You're a *good* person who deserves to be living your life."

I give myself a moment to digest everything he's said. I've spent so long being terrified of this plague that pretty much wiped out my generation of gay men. I knew things had changed drastically, and not only was it no longer a death sentence, but that people were living perfectly normal lives now.

However, to see Jack here in front of me confirms it for me in a way I hadn't appreciated I needed to see until now. I will never not be furious and devastated that Henry and countless others died so needlessly. But that Jack could ever think I'd resent the fact that he has access to life-saving medication is unbearable. I couldn't be more grateful in this moment for the incredible advancements in both treatment and prevention that we have today.

And on top of all that, he's telling me that he had an out and he *chose* to stay. Despite his rage and bitterness at what he thought I'd done, he took my deal to keep himself out of jail even if that meant sharing this space with me.

I would never turn him in now, though. Never.

I take a shaky breath. "I'm not sure I believe in an afterlife," I confess. "But there's this crazy thought in my head like Henry sent you to me. Jack, I…I know it's only been a few days, but I have to admit that I've become incredibly fond of you. It's like I didn't even know I had such a gaping void in my life until you showed up and turned everything on its head. It's as if I had to shake everything up to see it for what it truly was."

"Which is?" he asks.

"I was deathly afraid," I say, ripping off the plaster that's desperately been trying to salvage my broken heart for so long. "So I barricaded myself away from the world, thinking it would protect me. But this is no life. I want to live again, and…and I want to start that right now. With you."

"Felix?" he rasps, his shining eyes widening with what I pray is hope.

I tug at our already intertwined hands, yanking him to his feet before pulling him closer. I intended to get him standing between my knees, but in a flash, he's crawling into my lap.

And when his lips crash into mine, it truly feels like a gift from heaven.

CHAPTER 11
Felix

Jack might be small, but he's absolutely full of fight as he grips either side of my face and attacks my mouth with his own. I clasp either side of his ribs, my hands almost spanning the whole length of his torso as I dig my fingers into him.

Mine is all I can think. *Mine, mine, mine!*

"Felix," he moans against my lips, his tongue forcing its way deeper inside, tasting and teasing me.

My cock is rock hard in my trousers as he grinds his hips against me. If he's intimidated by my size, he hasn't given me a sign yet.

Good. Because I want to have him in every possible way imaginable.

But I know we'll have to start slow, no matter what my dick is demanding of me.

I move my hands, splaying one against his back and running the other through his hair, gripping it tightly. He whimpers, and lust shoots straight to my already straining cock.

Christ, he feels so fucking perfect, and I've only just got my hands on him. I'm definitely slightly hysterical with relief as I plunder his mouth over and over. I've been dreaming of this man every minute since he bulldozed into my life. But I hardly dared hope that he'd want me back with such intensity.

I want to give him *everything*. I want to wrap up all his hurt and anger and frustrations with this cruel world and smother them until all that's left is love and warmth and security. He's right that I shouldn't have to fear society anymore and have to stop hiding from it. But the same goes for him. He's been dealt some shitty cards. We both have. But I can quite literally physically and financially protect him from the woes that have plagued his and his mother's doors.

"Felix," he says again, and I fucking love the sound of it. As if he's claiming me. I feel feral, like a caveman, as I hastily shove my hands between our grinding crotches and start fumbling with his zip. He breaks our kiss and reaches down to help me.

In a flash, I seize his hand. I can feel my eyes blazing as they stare into his wide ones.

"*No*," I growl, my heart hammering in my chest. "*Mine.*"

He takes a few shaky breaths, then nods, his cheeks blushing beautifully. "Yours," he agrees.

I wrap my fingers around both his wrists and push his arms up, getting him to link his fingers behind my neck. "Here," I grunt. "Stay."

He nods again wordlessly, not moving as I capture his mouth once more and kiss him savagely. He wails and whimpers, but he doesn't move his hands.

Good boy.

He does, however, roll his groin against mine again, reminding us both of our very *hard* situation. I grin against his lips, loving how he can both be obedient as well as needy at the same time.

"*Yesss,*" he hisses as I resume my mission to unzip him and get my hand on his cock. He's unsurprisingly smaller than me there as well, but not so tiny that it gets lost when I wrap my fist around it. I begin to pump my hand, rubbing my thumb over his leaking slit. "Yes, Felix, *yes.*"

"Yes, Sir," I correct him.

My skin is tingling. I hadn't meant to ask that of him so soon, but he gulps and blinks his wide eyes for a second. "Yes, Sir," he repeats, the flush from his cheeks travelling down his neck.

"I'm in charge," I say gruffly. "I want to take care of you. I want to do everything for you. Is that okay?"

"So, *so* o-okay," Jack stammers. "I'm yours, Sir."

I grin and kiss him sloppily, adrenaline surging through my body. It took a long time to appreciate that I might not be any good at dating, but I'm damned good at dominating in the bedroom. Sure, it's been a while, and the last few occasions were paid for. But everybody had a sensational time. I always made sure of that.

However, now I have Jack, so sweet and small and pliant in my hands. He's perfect, so perfect. I watch in satisfaction as his eyelids flutter. I wank him off harder and rougher, desperate to see him come undone under my ministrations.

"Yes, please," he's begging, his voice weak and cracking with desperation. "Yes, Sir, please, *yes.*"

"Come for me, Jack," I tell him. "I want to watch you come, sweet boy."

He gnashes his teeth and drops his face against my neck. He starts screaming, and I love the fact that we can make as much noise as we want. There's no one this high who's going to hear us but the gods.

He starts spurting all over my hand, and I milk him for every drop, feeling a deep satisfaction that I haven't experienced in years. Jack trembles and gasps and clings to me for dear life until he collapses in a heap against me.

I chuckle and stroke the back of his damp hair. "Good boy," I murmur gently. "Such a good boy."

He hums and stays like that for a while until he lifts his head, blinking at me in a daze. "Your turn now, Sir," he says.

My grip on him tightens as he tries to wriggle away. "No," I rumble. "I said I was taking care of you, Jack."

He shakes his head, a mischievous glint in his eye. "If you think I'm leaving you without an orgasm, *Sir,* after you just made me come my brains out, you don't know me very well."

"No, Jack," I say firmly, but he's still pushing against me. He tucks his cock back in his underwear and manages to squirm between my legs where I'd originally planned on putting him.

Except right now, he's dropping to his knees.

"Stop me," he dares, and there's that passion, that fight that stirred my blood when I very first caught him in my vault.

"Jack, no," I warn him again. I think I sound convincing, but I don't mean it. If he wants to tousle with me, I'm game.

Very game.

"What are you going to do about it?" he asks giddily, slowly dragging my trouser zipper downwards.

"Punish you," I tell him honestly. My cock practically jumps in front of his face at the thought of it.

His breathing is ragged as he looks up at me through his lashes. "Will you spank me?" he whispers.

"Yes," I say back simply.

He lets out an obscene noise. "Promise?"

"Yes," I snarl.

He shivers and lunges for my cock, releasing it from my underwear. He must have had an idea of what he'd be facing because he doesn't flinch at the monstrosity of it. Most guys can guess from the size of the rest of me what they're getting into, but I have had a few baulk and run when faced with the actual reality.

Jack, however, looks like he hasn't just had a three-course meal.

He looks like he's starving.

I let out a guttural moan as he wraps his lips around it, swallowing me down as far as he can manage. Which isn't that far, but that's okay. I never expect anyone to be able to deepthroat it on their first try. It still feels fucking sublime as he sucks and slurps, wrapping his hand around the shaft and starting to stroke.

I thrust my hand into his hair and yank, not to particularly guide him, but just so he knows I'm there and still technically in charge. He squeaks at the pain, and it's so hot I can't help but thrust my pelvis up a little, making him choke and cough.

"Good boy," I say as he blinks away the tears and keeps right on sucking my giant cock. "Good boy, you look so fucking gorgeous."

He hums, moving his other hand from where he was steadying himself on my knee. Instead, he thrusts it inside my underwear, fondling my balls and stroking my taint. I drop my head back and grunt, trying to hold on as long as I can and not blow my load just yet.

But it's impossible. My cock has been on a hair trigger ever since Jack agreed to stay here, in my home. Sharing a space with him has been torture, and I've been incredibly restrained with not pleasuring myself to thoughts of something exactly like what's happening right now.

Watching Jack hungrily suck me off on his knees, drool dripping down his chin as he squeaks and moans, is filthier than any fantasy I could conjure with my own imagination. "Yes, yes, yes," I hiss as my climax races up to greet me, my eyes rolling into the back of my head.

He yelps as my cum starts hitting the back of his throat, instinctively trying to pull away. But I grab his hair and force him to take it all, loving how he hums and grips my legs, submitting beautifully to me.

As the last of my load pulses from my dick, I pull him off and enjoy how he gasps for air. He wanted my cock, so I gave it to him.

"Fuck, yes," he says hoarsely. "Holy shit. Yes, Sir. Thank you, Felix."

I manhandle him easily until he's back in my lap, kissing the hell out of his red and swollen lips. "You're mine, *mine*," I mumble into his mouth. "I never want you to leave, Jack. You belong to *me*." I'm talking nonsense, but he doesn't seem to care from the way he's kissing me back like it's his last act on Earth.

Lucky for him, it's not even his last act of the night. I'm not done with him yet.

Not by a long shot.

CHAPTER 12

Jack

I'M ONLY HALF-CONSCIOUS AS FELIX MANAGES TO REARRANGE himself once more so his trousers won't fall down. Then he bundles me up in his arms and fucking lifts me like I'm just a rag doll. I cling to him as we move back inside the penthouse, my eyes closed as I breathe him in.

It happened. It really happened. It's *still* happening.

Who knows how much time this bizarre arrangement is going to last for? But as long as I'm here, I want to be with Felix. The way he took charge just then was like something out of a dream, and in the state I'm in right now, I never want to wake up.

I realise that we've made our way to his bedroom, somewhere I haven't seen until now. Understandably, he wanted to keep some things private from the stranger who had barrelled his way into his life without permission. I expected it to be as carefully neutral as the rest of the place.

I was so wrong.

Unlike the monochrome tones of the rest of the space, it's got splashes of colour everywhere. Varying tones of blue and earthy greens are painted on the walls and run throughout the furnishings, paired with warm cream, brown, and bronze details in the large room. There are several pot plants with huge, holey leaves that are sat on every surface, clearly thriving. The art in the main living space is abstract and devoid of personality, in my humble opinion. But there are some sensual, gay AF portraits and studies hanging here.

And photos. As he sets me on my feet, I see the faces of what I assume to be friends and family, the images of Felix showing him significantly younger. One in particular is of him hugging a man with sandy-blond hair and something in me just knows that's Henry.

"Here you are," I say in wonder, shaking my head. He looks at me, and I wrap my arms around his waist, looking up at him. "I knew you were hiding yourself away somewhere, not just in that vault."

He looks around his bedroom like he's seeing it from a whole new perspective, and raises his eyebrows. "Huh," he says, giving me a lopsided grin. "I guess I have been hiding in here, haven't I?"

I shrug. "I'm glad I got to see it eventually. But maybe…"

"Maybe some of this stuff could be in the rest of the apartment as well?" he suggests.

I give him a cheeky grin. "Yeah, maybe."

I think about his other four properties. The stately home in Hampshire that his family have run for years. The beach house in California, the chateau in Marseille, and the massive condo in Singapore. Are they all just as lacking in personality? Or are they maybe just lacking in *Felix*, being so overwhelmed by the weight of the Fagiolo legacy? I guess I'll never know.

I'm soon distracted as he hums and leans down to kiss me. Holy *fuck*, for someone who's been avoiding people for a while, he really is a great kisser. And the way he took charge of my cock and the rest of my body…

Yeah, he's definitely not some shy recluse. If anything, I think I've unleashed a sexual deviant.

And I love it.

As if reading my mind, his hands travel down my back and squeeze my arse. "I believe I promised you a punishment," he murmurs in my ear.

I know I've only just come, and my stamina isn't what it used to be in my early twenties, but damn, my dick jumps excitedly at his words.

"Yes, Sir," I rasp, my voice still hoarse from how much of his delicious cock I was able to fit down my throat.

He slaps my arse, making me jump and laugh. "Off with those clothes then," he says in a no-nonsense tone.

"Bossy," I retort with a smirk, already stepping away and unbuttoning the fancy shirt he bought me.

"You only just noticed?" he says as he sits down on the side of the enormous bed.

If I thought the one I'd been sleeping in was nice, this is a whole other level. It's literally twice the size of my shitty one back at home, with black silk covers and sheets and about twenty different pillows. There's a dark wooden headboard with a space for a bronze bar running lengthways through the middle of it. It seems like a bit of a strange design feature, but I still like it, though.

I shake my head in response to his question as I continue my striptease. "I might have realised you like things your way when you literally kidnapped me and insisted on feeding and clothing me, Sir."

He grins, looking like the cat who found the cream. "Yeah, I love doing that shit," he says unabashedly.

I believe him. But not because he has some weird, nasty need to control stuff. But because he cares. He wants me to eat well and look good, and he gets a kick out of being able to make that happen.

I've fought for every damn thing in my life. I'd have never guessed that letting someone spoil me would be a turn-on. In fact, I would have bet against it. But Felix is just so damn cheerful about it all it's like I *want* to submit to him because I know it will be fun. That I'll enjoy it.

That he'll take care of me like no one ever has done before in my life.

I drop the shirt and toe off my shiny shoes before undoing my trousers and giving a little shimmy so they'll fall down my legs. I'm fully aware that I'm shaking my arse for him like an exotic bird in a mating ritual, but I don't give a shit. I've seen his gigantic cock, and I'm more than ready for the challenge of trying to get it inside me.

Speaking of birds, I'm grateful Goose seems to be elsewhere. As much as I love him, I don't really want a running commentary right now or a soundtrack of nursery rhymes.

I see there's cum on my trousers as I discard them, but I'm not embarrassed. I'm very thirsty for more, actually, as I peel off my socks and hook my thumbs under the waistband of my briefs. My eyes flick up to him, checking in.

"Do it," Felix grunts. Again, turning into a monosyllabic caveman wasn't on my radar of things that would turn me on. But the fact that I reduced his brain to some primal state before made me ridiculously proud, and now it's happening again.

I shuck them down and kick them away, leaving my hands by my hips as I breathe heavily, skin prickling with perspiration and tingling with anticipation. His eyes roam over my body hungrily. I think I'm in okay shape, but I'm especially proud of my tattoos, so I like the way his gaze lingers on them. I have a lot of the usual skulls and roses, other nature imagery, a few dedicated to my dad, as well as mythical creatures like gryphons and mermaids. However, my favourite is the phoenix rising from the ashes that takes up half my chest and winds around my side.

"Turn around," he instructs, and *fuck me,* that's so sexy. I've never had anyone inspect me like I'm some kind of prize pony before. But as I slowly rotate on the spot for him, I love the feeling of his eyes crawling over every inch of me.

What was it he said about his first love? How he made Felix feel like the centre of the universe?

Yeah. That's how I feel right now.

It's even better that he's still fully clothed. I feel so vulnerable and scared that my heart is in my throat. But I also know that he's going to look after me exactly like he's looked after me ever since he laid eyes on me. When I really, really didn't deserve it.

I hope I deserve it now. He's making me feel like I do.

He juts his chin in a clear command to come over. I go to stand in front of him, but in a flash, he grabs my hips and easily spins me like a pinwheel. I squeal, powerless as I end up on my front. My arms, head, and legs rest on the mattress, but my sensitive cock is jammed between his thighs, and my arse is up in the air. I try to catch my breath, and bunch my fists around the slippery duvet cover.

He brushes his hand over my head, carding his fingers through my hair. "You were naughty, Jack," he reminds me. "And now I'm going to punish you. You're going to endure it because I know you can. Then I'm going to take as long as I wish pleasuring you until I decide you can come. Do you understand?"

I'm quivering all over. I've always preferred bottoming and that generally meant the other guy would do more of the decision-making. But I've never had anyone actually take the decisions away from me. It should have made me rage and fight, but instead, I feel like fucking putty.

I don't know what on Earth possessed me to ask him to

spank me. It's not like I've really done that kind of thing before. I guess it was the way he took charge of my body, and it felt so good. I love the way he manhandles me and pulls my hair. I figure I've maybe looked at enough kinky shit online that I had the concept of spanking somewhere in the back of my mind. I must have wanted to try it, so when he suggested a punishment, the idea just slipped out.

There's not really any stopping it now, so I hope it's something I'll be into. We'll soon find out.

"Yes, Sir," I utter.

"Yes, what?"

I lick my lips. "Yes, I understand. Yes, I want it. *Sir.*"

He gives my hair a pull and hums. "Good boy. If it gets too much, you need a safe word. How about 'phoenix'?"

I let out a puff of laughter. I guess his favourite of my tattoos is the same as mine. I thought I caught him specifically checking it out just now. "Yeah, sure."

He pulls my hair again, lifting my hair and making me hiss. "And if you can't talk," he murmurs against my ear, his warm breath ghosting over my skin. "If your mouth is gagged or full of my massive cock, then you use your hand and tap three times wherever you can reach. If I have tied your hands, then you click three times. Understood?"

Holy fuck! Is he really going to tie me up? I picture myself helpless and bound whilst he does *whatever he wants with me,* and I'm suddenly squirming in his lap.

"Yes, yes," I pant desperately. "I understand, Sir. Please."

"Please, what?" he asks, still right by my ear, a savage purr to his words.

I take a shaky breath and realise there are tears in my eyes.

We were having such a raw and heartfelt conversation before we started making out like rabid beasts it's not surprising that my emotions are still close to the surface. I blink, feeling the wetness on my lashes, accepting it.

"Please do whatever you want with me," I whisper. *"Now."*

His hand comes crashing down on my arse without warning, and pain explodes through me, making me yell out. I gasp and instinctively try and move and get away, but Felix holds me firm. I take a few more breaths and settle down.

"Good boy, that's it," he praises me, and warmth blossoms in my chest, matching the heat already in my backside. "You can take it. Just let go, Jack. I'm going to push you to your limits. I'm in control. Just let go."

I can't find the words, so I just nod emphatically. I'm done questioning all the things I would never have considered consenting to before I met this man. I already feel like he knows me better than I know myself, so I'm going to do what he says and just take it.

And *whoa boy* does he give it.

He strokes my hair and rubs my back as he lands the first few stinging blows. I thought they were hard enough. But then he grips the back of my neck and starts up a steady string of hits across my arse cheeks and thighs. I cry and scream and jerk about like a worm on a hook, tears flowing down my cheeks. But he doesn't relent.

I'm not sure exactly when it happens, but the world around me becomes fuzzy and light. I feel like I'm floating. It's not like I can't feel the spanking anymore—far from it. But it's as if I become one with the pain, embracing it. Like it's lifting me up.

I have no idea how much time passes before he leans down and kisses the top of my head.

"It's over, Jack," he murmurs tenderly.

His large hands are caressing my fiery backside as well as my neck and shoulders. I turn my face from where it's been smashed into the mattress and sniff, hoping I'm not too disgusting after sobbing my heart out. If I am or not doesn't seem to matter. Felix nuzzles his nose against my cheek and presses lingering kisses wherever he can reach my skin with his mouth.

"You did so well for me. You were so perfect."

I'm apparently as fragile as a china doll because I burst into tears again. I'm vaguely aware as he gently moves me around so I'm on my side, cradled with my back to his chest. He's produced a hanky from somewhere and carefully mops me up.

"That's it, sweetheart," he murmurs against my ear as he lets me blow my nose. His words are no longer menacingly sexy but soothing and calm instead. "You did so well. Just let it all out."

He continues to hold me until my chest stops shuddering and my face stops leaking. The hanky is sodden by the time he drops it over the side of the bed, but I'm not embarrassed. I've never felt like this before. Like my chest has expanded and I can breathe properly without even knowing I'd been gasping for air this whole time.

"I want you to lie on your front now, Jack," Felix's voice rumbles through my bliss-filled haze. "I'm going to play with your body however I want. You're not allowed to come until I say so. Do you understand?"

I feel like I'm only half-conscious, but I manage to nod as I move on my front. "Yes, Sir," I rasp.

God, I want him to do everything to me. I want to be at his mercy. He's proved that I can trust him with that. He's also just shown me that he knows exactly how to push me to the edge and then bring me back safely.

"Are you going to tie me up?" I ask.

He stills next to my body. I blink and manage to look at him. He's regarding me curiously. "Would you like that?"

"You promised," I whisper. "I can click my fingers if I get in trouble."

His face is hard to read, but I think maybe he's proud. Does that make sense?

He cups the side of my face, caressing along my jaw with his thumb. "Of course I can do that, Jack. You wait here, and I'll take care of you."

I close my eyes, awash with calm. I feel it as he straps soft cuffs around my wrists, pulling my arms upwards. The bronze bar running through the headboard makes a lot more sense now as he attaches the other end of the cuffs to it. My heart is racing as my body tries to panic with the knowledge that I'm trapped, that I can't get away.

But another part of me knows that I've been trapped for days and made peace with that fact the second I accepted Felix's offer. My body belongs to him right now. He can do what he wants with it because all he wants is to make me feel good.

I trust him.

The restraints on my ankles are still padded, but I can tell immediately that they're way more restrictive. He's spread my legs out wide, and they're fixed that way. I'm able to take a peek over my shoulder and see there's a silver bar between them about a metre long attached to each cuff. I think it's called a spreader bar, for obvious reasons.

Whoa. Okay, I guess this is really happening.

I can't wait.

As I'm looking behind me, I notice that Felix's nice trousers are covered in a goopy mess. I think it must be pre-cum, but there's so much of it. "Did I come again when you were spanking me?" I ask incredulously.

He chuckles and turns away to rummage in a nearby drawer. "I had a feeling you didn't realise," he says, sounding positively gleeful. I have to give him credit. That's impressive. No wonder I feel boneless.

That doesn't mean I'm not going to be prepared for round three. Hell no.

I watch as he gets a couple of bottles out of the drawer—some lotion and lube. He looks intently at the back of the lube, and I realise he's checking it's still in date. That makes my heart ache both in fondness at how thoughtful he is but also with a little sadness.

If I had my way, he'd be running out of lube way before it was in any danger of expiring.

However, then he also pulls out a pretty normal-sized dildo, and my stomach drops with disappointment.

"You're not going to fuck me?" I blurt out.

As soon as I've spoken, I don't know if he's going to be a mean Dom and remind me that he promised he was going to play with my body however he wanted. Which is incredibly hot, don't get me wrong. But I'm glad when his face softens and he comes over to me, sitting on the edge of the bed, stroking the side of my face.

"Sweetheart, I'm huge," he says factually.

"Yeah," I reply, feeling less sleepy and more bratty by the second. "That's the point. I want it, now!"

He drops his head back and laughs. "If tying you up makes you this sassy, I'm going to have to do it again."

Okay, that mollifies me a little. We haven't even finished tonight, but I'm still desperate to talk about 'again' very soon.

I harumph, and he laughs once more. "I told you I was going to play with you. Now just lie there and take it. Or do I have to gag you?"

After a moment's consideration, I shake my head. This is still our first time as far as I'm concerned. Just one evening of a continuous string of orgasms. I want to be able to shout his name up to the high heavens so I can prove we're really here and—at least for now—I'm really his.

Felix moves behind me again "I promise, you'll enjoy it," he says.

I believe him, so I turn my head back around and get as comfy as I can when my shoulders are already starting to ache slightly, and my sensitive hole is exposed to the air.

I'm not sure what I was expecting, but I hiss when cold lotion hits the burning hot skin of my arse and thighs. The pain had dulled a little, but the cream feels like ice and Felix's strong hand is almost unbearable as he starts to massage it in.

I'm whimpering, and he shushes me. "It's okay, my little thief. It'll feel better in a second. Even though I do love the idea of beating you red and then making you take my cock after, that's a bit much for today."

Despite the fact that I'm in so much discomfort, that idea makes my cock jump under my belly against the mattress. Apparently, that sounds like fun to me, too. I'll just add it to the 'Who knew?' list.

I'm moaning, greedy for all the things I want from him. Things I have no right to because he's correct. I tried to steal from him.

I guess that's why now I'll take whatever he gives me, and I'll feel grateful for it.

So grateful.

The air is filled with the sweet floral scent of the lotion, and I have to admit that my behind feels a lot better now. Not that I want to be rid of the sting entirely. It's like a badge of honour I want to wear proudly. But I also want to be able to enjoy what comes next and not get distracted by anything else.

With my head turned into the pillow, it's almost like being blindfolded. I'm that much more keenly aware of all my other senses, so when he blows against my hole, I squeal and jerk in surprise. He chuckles darkly as he digs his fingers into the tender swell of my arse, pulling my cheeks apart so he can lick all the way up my crack.

Dear *lord*, I'm so pleased I cleaned myself out thoroughly before dinner.

I mewl and squirm as he leisurely eats me out, using his tongue and saliva to stretch and soften me up. His mouth feels divine on my most intimate area, and I make some truly filthy noises as he works me open.

By the time he's got two fingers in me, he's eagerly kissing and sucking my heavy balls. I'm slick with lube and spit, desperate to chase my third orgasm of the night. But every time I try and rut my cock against the bedding, he gives my flaming arse a light tap. It's so sore, though, that's all I need to scream and stop what I'm doing.

Each time he lets out a low, rumbling laugh and says, "Good boy."

Fuck, I want to be good for him so badly.

When he starts pushing in the dildo, I swallow it as fast as I can, loving when he turns the vibration on.

"Look at you," he purrs over me. "You're so wanton. You're going to be so ready for my cock when I give it to you. Fuck, you're all mine. I own you, Jack. You're *mine*."

I sob into the pillow, desperately trying not to grind down on my throbbing dick and find some release. Thankfully, Felix takes pity on me, although initially, it doesn't feel like it. He yanks my hips up, dragging my restrained feet up the bed as I rest on my knees, my cock straining in the cool air. He then switches off the vibration and stuffs the dildo inside me all the way up to its flared base, leaving it there. I turn my head to the side, blinking and wondering what's going to come next.

He grabs my hair and pulls my head up, making me look

back at him. I gasp at the pain but also at the sight of his enormous cock, slick with lube. I saw it before when I blew him, obviously. But now he's got his trousers and underwear around his thighs, and he's furiously wanking himself off, the big mushroomy head rubbing against my hole and thighs and the base of the dildo.

He keeps a grip on my hair like he's a cowboy riding his horse. I'm helpless to do anything but pant and whimper as he uses me to get himself off.

I love it.

With a bellow, he suddenly starts shooting thick white ropes of cum all down my back and splattering along my thighs. He comes and comes, gnashing his teeth but never taking his eyes off me.

In that moment, I really am his whole world.

When he finally empties his balls completely, he lets go of my hair and grabs my hip to steady himself. But he's three times my size, so I just sort of sink into the bed, and he laughs.

"Sorry, sweetheart," he says.

He's dripping with sweat, face flushed, clothes damp, limbs heavy with exhaustion. It's the most gorgeous I've seen him look so far.

He reaches up and does something with the cuffs above my head. I feel like they're sliding to the middle maybe, giving my arms slack so they're no longer stretched. But then he takes hold of my sides, and before I know what's happening, he flips me onto my back.

I shriek, and he grins, immediately leaning down to kiss my mouth. "You're so fucking cute," he mumbles against my lips. "My own little plaything. Such a good boy."

My body is a trembling wreck, and my mind is mush. So all I can find the strength to utter is, *"Please.* Please, Sir."

"It's okay, Jack," he says against my skin as he kisses down my neck and then my chest. "I've got you, sweetheart. I'm going to take care of you. I promised. You can come whenever you like now. But I'd really like it if you could hold out until I tell you to do it."

I whine, tears sliding down either side of my face as he kisses along my tummy and tickles my flanks with his big, blunt fingers. My cock jerks and bobs, spitting pre-cum, but Felix ignores it for the moment as he licks and kisses along my hips and on the inside of my thighs.

"*Please*, Felix," I beg.

The use of his name makes him sigh sweetly and rest his cheek against my leg, looking up the length of my body at me. "Jack," he says like he's uttering a prayer. "Say my name again, gorgeous."

"Felix," I moan. "Felix, *Felix!*"

When his lips finally wrap around my bright red and throbbing member, I don't hold back. I'm not big at all, so I fuck up into his mouth with abandon, thrashing against my restraints and screwing up the bed covers.

"Fuck, Felix, yes! Fuck!"

He pushes against the dildo still jammed inside me, turning the vibration back on so it massages my prostate. Then he wraps his hand around my balls and squeezes, all while he's swallowing me down beyond his tonsils.

I scream his name, clinging desperately onto my climax, determined not to come until he tells me to. I *want* this. I *can* hold on. But he certainly tortures me, sucking relentlessly for another minute or so. I have no idea—time means nothing anymore.

Eventually, he slides up my shaft, coming off with a little pop. I stare into his eyes which are burning with intensity as he wraps his fingers around my cock and begins to pump.

"Come for me, little thief. Give me everything."

I screw my eyes shut and arch my back, thrusting into his

hand as my orgasm rips through me, robbing me of breath and sight. I don't know how long I come all over myself, but it feels like forever. Considering this is my third time in so many hours, it's safe to say that when I collapse into a heap, I am thoroughly and completely spent. Empty. Devoid of anything except the dizzying bliss that's consumed me.

The bed dips as Felix crawls up my body. He cups my face and kisses my lips softly. "Good boy," he whispers. "My good boy."

Nothing else matters to me in that moment, and I'm not sure when it will again.

I just want to be his. And good.

But mostly, *his.*

CHAPTER 13

Felix

JACK IS AN ABSOLUTELY GLORIOUS MESS UNDERNEATH ME. I'M shattered as well, but he's practically comatose after everything I just put him through.

It couldn't have been more perfect.

I pull my trousers back up. Then I undo the cuffs around his wrists and ankles very carefully, massaging those areas as well as his shoulders to make sure the blood is flowing like it should. I take a look at the cut on his palm from yesterday as the plaster is peeling off. It looks like it's closed up nicely, so I pull the plaster off to allow the wound to air and heal better.

He hums and whimpers as I move him around, muttering something unintelligible as I collect him in my arms and carry him into the en suite. I prop him up on the closed toilet seat and wrap a big towel around him. "Jack? Can you hear me?" He blinks his eyes open and smiles sweetly at me. "Good boy," I say, brushing the backs of my fingers against his cheek. "Can you stay here for a minute for me?"

"Yes, Sir," he croaks.

I love how wonderfully he took my orders. That's what I

wanted in the heat of the moment. But now I want to hear my name on his lips again.

"Can you call me Felix now?" I ask gently. "I like Sir for sexy times, but for the rest of the time, it just sounds so nice when you use my name."

"Felix," he says, reaching out and cupping his small hand against my face.

I sigh and lean into the touch just for a second. But I have to take care of him right now. Everything else is secondary.

"Stay here and don't fall asleep," I warn him. The last thing I need is for him to topple over and crack his head open on the sink or something.

"Promise," he says, crossing over his heart.

I press a chaste kiss to the corner of his mouth, then run from the bedroom back down to the kitchen. I gather up some bottled water and biscuits. I don't have any sports drinks on hand. I wasn't expecting an epic sex session, not even in my wildest dreams. But I do have juice, so that will do for now.

I sprint back upstairs and am stupidly relieved to find Jack exactly where I left him. "Good boy," I say breathlessly, pleased when he gives me a little smile.

"Fuck, I'm tired, Felix," he grumbles, making me laugh.

"There he is. My little grumpy thief." I hold out the half-finished bottle of fresh orange juice. "Drink all of this, please," I say kindly but also in my no-nonsense voice.

He just hums and takes it from me, downing several gulps in one go.

"Excellent," I tell him honestly. "Now I want you to eat at least three chocolate digestives for me. Can you do that?" I place the biscuit packet next to him and watch as he slowly pulls the top one out and has a nibble. "Brilliant. Okay, three, remember? I'll be back in a minute."

He takes another bite, so I dash through the door again.

This time I stay in the bedroom, observing the damage. The bed might be rumpled but we actually kept all our antics on top of the duvet. So I collect up my equipment and put it all back in the cupboard where my larger kinky stuff lives, then yank the duvet cover off to throw into the wash tomorrow. It doesn't take long to put a new one on from the cupboard, then the bed looks nice and cosy again.

I have no intention of letting Jack sleep in the spare room tonight. I'm keeping him close by.

"This is number three," Jack says almost combatively as I step back into the bathroom, making me laugh.

"I trust you," I tell him as I ruffle his hair. I also notice that the juice has all gone as well, and I'm satisfied. "Okay, it's definitely bedtime. Let's get cleaned off, hmm?"

He nods as he finishes his last biscuit, brushing the crumbs from his hands. I get the water running in the shower, as I think that'll be the quickest option tonight. I'd love to lounge in the bath with him, but I'm pretty sure we'd both pass out.

I strip off my clothes and throw them into the laundry basket as well. I can fetch the things Jack dropped on the floor in a minute.

He snorts as he looks up at me, still punch-drunk. "You're so fucking gorgeous," he slurs.

I grin and lean down for a kiss before ushering him under the water, moving the nozzle down so it doesn't miss him entirely. "So are you. I want to hear the stories behind all these tattoos someday."

He beams as I squirt shampoo on top of his head. "You like them?"

"I love them, sweetheart," I tell him honestly. "They're beautiful. Just like you."

He just hums happily and lets me wash him. It's almost comical how the water stream can't accommodate us both, but I prioritise him, then manage to give myself a quick rinse by removing the head and holding it above myself.

Once the suds are all gone, I switch off the water and grab the same towel I just wrapped Jack up in for him to have again. He clumsily dries himself as I hastily rub another towel over my own body. Once I'm not dripping anymore, I drop it back on the heated rail and take over from Jack, gently drying his hair.

"Thank you," he whispers.

"You're welcome," I tell him back.

Normally, I set a timer to brush my teeth, but tonight I just give them a quick seeing to and insist Jack does the same with another spare I had in my cupboard. I couldn't be arsed to run down and get the one he's been using, and silently thank my housekeeper for always stocking up this place so well.

I grab the water bottles and lead us out of the bathroom. We're both naked as I sit him on the edge of the bed. He looks fresher but still exhausted. "Shall I go get you some underwear or pyjamas?" I ask him.

I didn't want to leave him for his toothbrush, but it's occurred to me that this is important. If we were definitely having sex again, I'd just tell him I wanted him naked. But I don't want him to feel pressured into anything in the cold light of the morning. I offer him the choice so he'll be most at ease.

He shakes his head, though. "Can we be naked?" he asks, a sparkle of mischief in his eyes despite the fact that he's barely clinging to consciousness.

"Of course, sweetheart," I say with a chuckle. "Come on. Let's get snuggled in."

I pull the covers back for him and get him lying down against the pillows. Once he's tucked in, I do a quick dash to pick up his clothes, not minding they'll get mixed up with mine in the wash. In fact, it feels ridiculously domesticated, and I love it.

I turn the overhead light off, just leaving my bedside lamp on so I can navigate my way back to the bed. As soon as I get in and switch it off, Jack wriggles up to me so he's the very little spoon to my big one. I sigh contentedly as I wrap my arms around him and draw him as close as I can to be.

I love that he didn't even question where he would sleep tonight. He knows he's mine.

At least for now.

"Goodnight, my little thief," I murmur, pressing a kiss just behind his ear.

"Not a thief," he grumbles, even though there's no real malice to his words. "Didn't steal anything in the end, remember?"

He's practically asleep before the last word tumbles from his mouth, so he probably doesn't hear me chuckle. He might still feel the second kiss I place on his cheek or notice the way I stroke his warm skin, even if it's just subconsciously.

In the quiet and the dark, doubt creeps at the edge of my mind. How long can I realistically keep him here? He's mine for the moment, sure, but for how long? I don't want to dwell on it, but facts are facts. This is a fantasy right now. How will it measure up once reality seeps back in? Are we actually compatible, or is this just a type of Stockholm syndrome?

I seriously hope not. I want to tell him he can leave any time he wants, coin collection be damned. I want to know he's here because he *wants* to be.

He's right. I should stop calling him my little thief. He didn't actually take anything and unless this is some incredible long con, I sincerely doubt he's secretly a gold digger.

But as I lie there, waiting for sleep to claim me, I realise he is in fact wrong about that. He says he's not a thief, that he didn't steal anything. But that's not true.

He stole my heart the moment he came crashing into my life. And now there's a very strong chance that I won't get it back.

Because I don't want it. I'm pretty sure I want him to keep it.

CHAPTER 14

Jack

If I thought I'd been sleeping like the dead in the other bed, that's nothing to how I feel when I wake up in Felix's bed the next morning. I'm sure it has everything to do with the insane quality of the mattress and pillows and nothing to do with the triple orgasm fuck fest.

I giggle to myself as I stretch and rub my eyes. But then I'm suddenly hissing as I roll over and put pressure on my arse and thighs.

I still grin, though. I'm proud of how I took that punishment. I always thought spanking was a kind of 'tee-hee' activity you just added in occasionally during vanilla sex. I never knew it could make me fly like that. That it could be something in and of itself that two people could share together.

I know Felix got off on administering the blows as much as I did taking them. He might not have orgasmed unaware like yours truly, but it definitely made him satisfied in ways I'll probably never understand.

"What are you so pleased about," a rumbling voice asks beside my ear. Felix is snaking his arms around me again from where we moved apart in the night, pressing kisses to my neck, jaw, and cheek.

I turn so he can capture my lips. "Thinking about last night," I mumble into his mouth.

He hums happily. "Good."

"Good? It was bloody excellent," I protest.

He laughs and starts tickling me, presumably having worked out how much I like that during round two of our adventures. I'm immediately gasping and squealing, trying to get away, even though it's making me hard and dizzy.

"You're so sensitive," he says against my throat as he relents and hugs me again. "I love that."

"Yeah?" I ask just because I want to hear more about the things he loves about me.

He nods and kisses my pulse point. "Lots of possibilities for fun there, little one."

He called me little thief several times last night. I protested, but I actually liked it. I'm sure not many people meet their lovers in that way. I don't mind being reminded of my almost crime, because it all worked out okay in the end.

It brought us together.

I like him calling me his little one as well, though. I hope it's not fetishising or anything, but I think the size difference between us is fucking hot. Especially having experienced it whilst actually…well…fucking.

I know I need to get up and take my pill, not to mention that I kind of need the loo. But when Felix starts kissing me, I'm powerless to resist. I congratulate myself on my sleepy decision for us to go to bed naked last night because when he climbs on top of me and presses me against the mattress, his huge, slippery cock rubs freely against my small one, and it's utter bliss.

Maybe I can wait a little longer to start my day.

A few hours later, I am showered, fed, and back at work in the safe putting Felix's beloved coin collection back together. The more time I've spent on it, knowing its significance to him, the less it's felt like a chore and the more it's become a passion project. I want to give him this gift.

However, we can't deny that something monumental has shifted between us since last night, and something is nagging at me. So much so that after an hour or two, I get restless enough to abandon my post and head back up to my room to fetch something.

As Felix wasn't working with me that morning, I go hunting through the penthouse for him. I feel like I've earned permission to do that now after being invited into his bedroom for the entire night. But I obviously don't go snooping around. I just want to find him to talk to him.

Eventually, I find him on the top floor. I haven't seen any of the other rooms up there aside from Felix's, but this door leads me into a gorgeous study. The walls are lined with floor-to-ceiling bookcases and there are even more plants in here than his bedroom. A massive, gleaming wooden desk dominates the centre of the room—unsurprising given Felix's stature. But that's not where I discover him.

He's lounging on a plush, velvet sofa to my right. He looks up from the book he's reading, which appears to be a biography of someone I've never heard of. But the way he blinks and then smiles at me is so cute I don't really care about anything else.

"Hey, sweetheart," he says, sounding delighted to see me. I blush. No one's ever delighted to see me, except maybe my mum. "Is everything okay?"

I nod, stepping inside the room. Movement to the right catches my eye, and I flinch. But then I let out a relieved laugh as I realise it's just Goose stretching his wings. "Hello, hello," he squawks. "Pretty boy, breakfast, breakfast, eat up, *ohhh, Felix, Felix!*"

If I was blushing before the pet parrot *imitated my sex moaning,* I think I pretty much burst into flames on the spot afterwards. "Uhh…" I croak.

Felix—the bastard—howls with laughter, covering his face with his book. "He's got you down to a T."

"Shut up," I mumble to them both. I was nervous enough coming up here, and now I've had to suffer a bloody bird mocking me, my insides are feeling a little like jelly. But I came up here with a mission, and I'm going to see it through.

Felix takes pity on me. He jams a bookmark in between the pages and places the biography down on a side table. "Come here, little one. Don't let that silly Goose bully you."

"Why *is* your parrot called Goose?" I ask him as I make my way over to the sofa.

He pulls me down and tucks me against his side. I'm glad I just asked him a question because I turn into useless goo for at least a minute after that. God, I could stand to be cuddled like this all the time. I know that's a fantasy, but I let myself indulge in it for now, at least. Even my sore bum is part of the dream, which I never would have guessed before last night.

"His real name is Benjamin," Felix explains, trailing his fingers up and down my arm, making me shiver. It's astonishing how fast he's got into showing me casual physical affection. I love it, but it is also taking me a minute to wrap my head around it.

"Benjamin?" I repeat. Goose doesn't react at all. He just continues nibbling at his feathers.

Felix nods. "My mother bought him for me as a present a little while after Henry passed. I don't think it ever once occurred to her what the true nature of our relationship was, but she knew I was sad because my friend had died. So she surprised me with Benjamin. Eclectus parrots can live up to fifty years, you know?"

"Wow, really?"

He hums. "My family never does anything by halves," he says with a chuckle. "I was so deeply heartbroken and lost in severe depression, but Benjamin wasn't having any of that. He quickly became my own personal clown and wouldn't stop messing around until I laughed. I called him a silly goose whenever he did, and by the time I managed to crawl my way back to reality, Goose had become his name."

The bird bobs on his perch at hearing his name mentioned. "Silly Goose, good boy, pretty boy."

I blush yet again as I try not to get jealous *of a parrot*. But I very much liked being Felix's 'good boy' last night.

"So your family doesn't know you're gay?" I ask.

Felix shakes his head. "They never did, no. They both passed in the last five years. I came to them late in life, so not only were they more like grandparents in age than parents, but they were also staunchly conservative. They loved me dearly, though, and I had so little of that in my life, so I wanted to cling to that. I didn't want to risk losing them." He sighs. "It made me a coward."

"Hey, no," I say crossly. I angle my head so we can look at one another. "That doesn't make you a coward. You were just protecting yourself. You suffered a devastating bereavement at such a young age. It makes perfect sense that you wouldn't want to risk any more loss."

He shrugs and looks at Goose. "I wish they could have known the real me. Met Henry. Hell, I'm still not really *out* out. I have friends who know but I swear my board thinks I'm some sort of eccentric monk."

I can't help but laugh at that, and I'm pleased when he

smiles back at me. "I don't think monks are allowed to have sex," I whisper conspiratorially.

His grin widens. "Ah, I knew I was going wrong somewhere."

He kisses me on the mouth then sighs again. "Anyway, it's not like I've even had a proper relationship since Henry, which is a little sad. But at least I haven't had to hide anyone away like a mistreated heroine in a gothic novel."

He laughs, but I have to wonder—does that mean he'd hide me away?

Urgh. Spriggs, stop that. We're not dating. We just had sex a few times. Yeah, it was spectacular, but I need to stop envisioning it as some long-term thing.

"Anyway, what about you?" he asks. I blink, not following. "Are you out to your family?"

"Oh, right," I say, smiling fondly. "Yeah. That's something I'm really fucking glad of. I got to tell my dad before we lost him. He was fine with it. Said as long as I was happy, that was all that mattered."

I resist the urge to roll my eyes at how *unhappy* I became for several years after his death, but I still have time to honour that promise I made to him.

"My mum's always nagging at me to bring a nice man home," I say instead with a laugh. "She doesn't care in the slightest. She *does* care when I get up to off the books shenanigans, so I really should knock that shit off for the sake of her nerves. Speaking of which…"

It's the perfect segue, so I take it before I can chicken out. I fish into my pocket and pull out the three different coloured fobs, holding them out for Felix to see.

"What are those?" he asks.

I know he saw them before, but I have a feeling he wants me to explain them, whether or not he already knows the answer. That's fair, and I want to. Our relationship started on completely the wrong footing. I have no idea how long I'll be able to stay here with him in this fantasy bubble of ours. But whilst I'm here, I don't want to be keeping secrets.

"Magic beans," I say with a chuckle, but my heart feels heavy, and it quickly dies in my throat. I sigh and pick up Felix's large hand, tipping the fobs from my palm to his. "They're how I broke into here. One for the building, one for your front door, and one for the safe. It didn't feel right keeping them."

He curls his hand around them, capturing my hand as well. For a minute, we just sit there quietly, looking at our joined hands. Then he kisses my neck and nuzzles his nose against my cheek, and I can breathe again. I take it he's not mad, then.

"Thank you for being honest," he says. "Everyone fucks up, Jack. The important thing is to admit when we do and to grow from it."

I drop my head and rest our temples together. "How are you so nice? So kind and forgiving? Pretty much anyone else would have had me in police custody days ago."

"It's a good job I'm not like most people, then, isn't it?" he says playfully.

I smile and lean in for a kiss. "You definitely are not, Felix Fagiolo."

We make out for a little bit before he breaks off and frowns. "Seriously, though. Is my security that shit?"

I burst out laughing and shake my head. "No, my friend is just a literal genius at these things. If I were you, I'd hire him to fix all the weaknesses he found. Then no one on the planet will be able to break in here ever again."

Felix hums, not sounding convinced. The frown looks so wrong on his face that I poke it. Immediately, he blinks and laughs at me.

"That's better," I say. "You're supposed to be the cheerful one. I'm the grumpy one."

"Yes, but you're *my* grumpy one," Felix says playfully.

I know he's just messing around, but I do wish I really could be his.

He drops the fobs on the coffee table, and then there isn't much more talking after that. I don't want to give Goose more ammunition to tease me with, after all.

I might not ever be the cheerful one, but after my confession, I certainly feel lighter than I have in a very long time. I don't know what this thing between us could ever be long-term in the real world. It seems so unlikely and implausible. But at least for the duration of my time here, I want our relationship to be honest. It started with hatred and confusion for me, but I want that to be in the past now. If Felix is okay with everything, then so am I.

The past is in the past. I might not know what the future holds, but I'm determined to make the most of the present.

For however long it lasts.

CHAPTER 15

Felix

EVENTUALLY, I LET JACK GET BACK TO WORK AFTER OUR FUN IN the study. I have this wild idea about fucking him in every single room of the penthouse. Sadly, though, my mind is distracted from such a lovely daydream by something nagging me.

Despite his assurances that his friend is some sort of technological prodigy, I'm still quite perturbed that someone was able to just give Jack three little fobs, and that meant he could walk his way right into my safe. If he'd been a douchebag, he could have stolen some of my most precious possessions. He could have wrecked my home.

He could have pretty easily un-alived me if I hadn't heard him come in.

Last week, I probably wouldn't have been that disturbed by the idea. What was I really living for, anyway? Some days, the thought of how lonely, confused, and heartbroken Goose would get was the only thing keeping me going. I've just been coasting aimlessly for years.

But then Jack came crashing into my life and reminded

me of how I swore to Henry that I'd live for us both. That I'd keep going when he couldn't.

I need to live for myself, I know. But I can't stop from thinking that Jack could be something worth living for as well. Is that crazy? It's only been a few days. Yet my grumpy little thief lights up my home in a way I'm not sure it ever has been. He doesn't just make my heart beat, he makes it pound and throb and ache. I haven't felt this awake in years. I don't just want to hide up here in my ivory tower anymore. I want to feel connected to this big, beautiful world.

However, I can't deny that even if it's only been a short time, Jack's well-being has very quickly become a top priority for me. So I keep rolling the three fobs around in my hand, wondering yet again how it happened that our paths crossed in such an unlikely set of circumstances. I'm not talking about why he decided to target me—we've long since put that to bed, even if I do still feel guilty for my negligence.

No, there's something else on my mind.

"This must be a really good friend of yours," I say by way of announcing my presence at the safe door. Jack blinks and looks up from the Japanese mon he's got between his fingers.

"Hmm?"

I hold up one of the fobs. "This friend of yours just gave these to you, did he?"

Jack's ears go a little pink, but not in the usual adorable way. He looks shifty as he drops his gaze back to the old coin he's handling in his gloved-up fingers. "Um, yeah, sure."

I arch an eyebrow. "Really? You didn't have to pay for them?"

This is what's bothering me. I don't like the idea of Jack struggling for money when I literally have more than I know what to do with ten times over. If he got himself into debt trying to right what he thought was the wrong I'd done his family, I can't let that lie. I want to pay him back. But first, I need to find out just how much trouble he got himself into.

"Um, no," Jack says. "Not exactly."

I lean against the doorframe and stare at him until he looks up again. He sighs when he sees my expectant face. We literally just talked about owning our mistakes and the importance of honesty, and he knows it. We're both acutely aware that he broke into my home, and that's all fine now. So long as he's not keeping things from me any longer.

"I was supposed to give him a cut once I sold the things I ripped off from you," Jack says miserably. My heart aches for him. I know he's a little shit for trying to steal from me in the first place, but it's easy to see how remorseful he is now.

"And he trusted you wouldn't rip him off as well?" I ask bluntly.

Jack shrugs, rolling the coin around between his thumb and finger. It's easy to see it's a mon by the square cut into the middle of it. "He, um, took something from me for insurance. Something he knew I'd have to come back for."

I think about that for a second. "So he still has this item of yours. The insurance."

Jack deliberately doesn't look at me. "It's fine. Whatever. I'm obviously not robbing you now, so I'll find another way to pay him back. He wasn't being malicious, just practical. I do fully intend on paying him for his services."

"How much?" I ask.

Jack shakes his head. "Twenty percent of whatever your stuff fetched. I guess he'll name his price now, and knowing him, it'll be a big one, and he'll have me wriggling on a hook for years paying him off." He laughs hollowly, but I don't find it all that funny.

"Well, I'll just pay him," I say. That makes Jack look up sharply at me.

"Absolutely not," he snaps.

"Why not?" I ask, genuinely confused. "It's just money that's sitting around not doing anything. I don't like the idea of this bloke holding on to something important to you, friend or not."

Jack bounces his knee where he's sitting. "Because that's… I don't know. Vulgar or something. I don't like the idea of you doing that. It's wrong. You're the victim in this situation. Having you pay out just feels awful to me."

I don't mean to laugh, but it comes out anyway. "Jack, I hate to be crass, but it'll probably be peanuts to me. I told you I want to look after you. Let me do this for you. What is it this friend of yours is keeping from you? We can—"

"Felix, I said *no*," Jack growls, bringing me up short. Then he sighs, his shoulders sagging. "I tried to hurt you. I'm so ashamed of that now. I…I care about you. I can't use you for your money after that, even if you want to give it freely. It feels cheap. I don't…this isn't cheap, the thing we have now."

I bite my lip and nod. "I couldn't agree more," I say, coming into the vault and sinking to my knees beside him. "Which is why I want to take care of you. But I respect what you're saying, and I won't mention it again."

For now, I add mentally. When he's less raw, I'm hoping he'll see reason. There's no way I'm just going to let him suffer, even if by his reasoning, he brought it upon himself.

"Thank you," he mumbles, leaning into me. I wrap my arm around him and hug him tightly. "I'm sorry to be such an arse about it."

I chuckle. "I wouldn't have it any other way, my little grumpy one. Thank you for being honest, even if it's not what I wanted to hear. That means a lot to me."

He nods against my chest. "I'll always be honest with you, Felix. I promise."

"Good boy." I brush another kiss against his hair.

I kiss the top of his head, loving the way he smells like my products. He's slotted so easily into my life here. It feels right.

I don't want to think about what will happen when he leaves.

If. *If* he leaves. I know everything about how we met is absurd and, in many ways, we are vastly different human beings. But isn't that what keeps relationships interesting? Henry and I were nothing alike, really, and I still loved him with the passion only a teenager could manifest.

I want to feel that kind of love again. I want to wake up each morning knowing that I am a part of something bigger than just myself.

I want the time to find out if I could be falling in love with Jack.

So, no. He's not going anywhere for the foreseeable future if I get my way. He's in between jobs and wouldn't need to work anyway if he was with me. It's clear he's not lazy by the way he's thrown himself into restoring my coin collection. But without the crushing pressure of paying the bills looming over his head, perhaps he could discover what truly captures his heart and his imagination.

But I need to be patient.

I know this is hard for him to trust someone new. Hell, it's hard for me, too. It might feel natural to swoop Jack up and have him in my life overnight, but it's been a long time since I shared this much time and space with anyone. I need to respect boundaries and remember that we're going to go through things at different paces. I can't let my desire to protect him and care for him lead me into steamrolling over what he actually wants and needs.

But that's okay. We'll keep talking, keep moving forwards together. It might have been fast, but I'm all in. I can see this growing bigger and stronger into a real, long-term relationship. But I can't scare Jack off before we've even begun.

That's okay, though. I've waited all this time for him. I'm in no rush. I can wait a little longer.

And in the meantime, I can think of *plenty* of things to keep us occupied.

Oh, yes.

CHAPTER 16

Jack

"ARE YOU DONE FOR THE DAY?"

I look up to see Felix hovering in the doorway of the safe again. Unlike this morning, when he was pensive and anxious, he's practically giddy now, rocking on the balls of his feet, his hands clasped behind his back like he's trying to contain himself.

I look around. The space is so much less messy than it was before. I feel proud. "Um, I was going to try and get a couple more coins homed at least—" I begin.

"Nope," he interrupts. "You're done. Come on." He grins, and I can't help but laugh.

"Okay, then," I concede, pulling my latex gloves off and rising to my feet. I wince a little after sitting so long on my still-tender arse, but honestly, I quite enjoy the sensation. "Is dinner ready?" I can't smell anything, but it might be something cold, or he might have ordered in again.

Or it might be none of those things.

He shakes his head and beckons me over with his fingers. "We can eat later," he says.

That's all the warning I get before he throws his hands under my sore bum and hoists me into the air. I yelp, slinging my arms around his neck and wrapping my legs around his solid torso.

"Hi," I say breathlessly, enjoying being face to face for once. His eyes are such a beautiful shade of blue, like the sky that surrounds us here up in the clouds.

"Hi," he says devilishly. "I missed you."

I roll my eyes, but I'm still grinning. "I've been right here all day."

"Exactly," he says with a pout, "and that's nowhere near my bed. So I decided to rectify that."

I'd laugh, except he captures my mouth for a filthy kiss. Any protest I might have had melts away as I deepen the kiss, snaking my arms and legs tighter around his body like a python.

It's been troubling me how far I am along with restoring the coin display. Not to mention I've only got a couple of days left worth of meds. I don't know how much longer I'll be able to stay in this magical wonderland, so I'm very keen to make the most of it.

We make our way up the two flights of stairs with me still glued to his mouth, and I have to marvel at not just his strength but his balance as well. I'm doing my very best to distract him, after all. But eventually, we find our way to his bedroom, and he nips my lower lip before placing me back on my feet.

I'm already feeling light-headed, and sway on the spot for a second. But then I blink and glance around the room, immediately realising something has changed.

In fact, several things have changed.

My jaw drops as I take in the hundred flickering tea lights he's placed around the room. The bed is covered in red rose petals. On one of the nightstands stands the ornate silver ice bucket with a fresh bottle of Champagne, as well as a bowl of strawberries and a pot of liquid chocolate.

On the other nightstand is an old-fashioned duster—the kind with a short wooden handle and a plume of black ostrich feathers. I also see a metal pinwheel with plenty of sharp needle points and a fat red wax candle with a lighter sat next to it.

And in the middle of the foot of the bed is a basket filled with soft-looking black ropes.

My knees go weak as my pulse quickens. I might not have played around with much kinky stuff before, but I do have access to the internet.

"Are you going to tie me up again?" I whisper, clinging to Felix's side for support.

He wraps a strong arm around me and kisses the top of my head. "Yes, little one. You're mine, and I'm going to make sure you can't get away. We're going to play with all that lovely sensitive skin of yours."

I nod, my mouth feeling dry, even though Felix has been an absolute tyrant about keeping me hydrated all day. Probably because he had plans all along to wring me out again.

I always thought it was a bit weird that I kind of... well...*got off*...on the pain I felt during my many tattoo sessions. I never told a soul about it, certainly not Felix. But as I look at the pinwheel sitting innocuously by the bed, I realise he's perhaps figured out something about me quicker than I ever did.

"Do you need to use your safe word, Jack?"

I shake myself and look at his concerned face. I must have been still and thinking for a bit too long. "No, Sir," I say breathlessly. "I was just feeling a little...overwhelmed, I guess? This all looks so exciting. But, um..."

"New?" Felix suggests, and I nod, turning my body against him, feeling shy. He chuckles and rubs my back. "That's okay, little one. I like that this is something I can show you that no one else has before. It just makes me feel like I own you even more."

It's funny that his money talk earlier freaked me the fuck out. But when he says that my body belongs to him now and he can do whatever he likes with it, that's like an electric pulse straight to my cock.

"Come here," he says, pulling me towards the bed. He perches on the edge and drags me between his legs. I love being manhandled by him like a doll, which is good, as he wastes no time in putting his hands all over me.

Thick fingers work lightning fast to pull my jumper off and undo my jeans, stripping me down until I'm totally naked. I get that thrill again from him still being dressed, and I sense he feels it too from the way his eyes are drinking me in.

He settles himself with his back against the pillows, then tugs me down into his lap, tucking me under his wing again like he did in his study this morning, and my pulse quickens. I feel so small and protected but also kind of trapped, which I strangely like.

That's probably a good thing, given the theme of the evening.

He reaches out for a juicy strawberry from the bowl, dipping the tip into the runny chocolate. He doesn't seem to care when it drips on the sheet that he's laid over the duvet, and certainly not when it gets on my chest. I suspect that's the whole point of the exercise, in fact.

He holds it up to my mouth, and without saying a word, I bite into it, the tangy flavour of the fruit bursting over my tongue. Combined with the rich chocolate, I can't help but moan at their deliciousness. "Good boy," he murmurs against my ear, and I shiver all the way down to my toes.

He feeds me several more before touching my chin to

turn my head so he can kiss my mouth thoroughly. He laps up every last morsel of sweetness from my lips and tongue, then he scoots over on the bed, making the petals flutter over the covers.

"Lie down, sweetheart," he tells me, and I do, getting my head comfy on the pillows. Then I sigh and whimper as he proceeds to lick off every drop of chocolate that's fallen down my chest and even the few splashes that caught on my thighs. "Delicious," he declares, looking up at me with a mischievous sparkle in his eyes. "I'm going to tie you up now, little thief. Just lie back and relax. I'll take care of you."

"Yes, Sir," I say with a sigh.

He starts by taking a pair of scissors with rounded tips and placing them on the nightstand by the red candle. "If we get into trouble," he explains to me, holding my gaze steadily, "you just say the word, and I can cut you free. Understood? I don't care about the ropes. I care about you."

Gosh, that does tingly things to my heart. "Yes, Sir."

"Good boy."

He starts with my wrists, using the silky rope to bind them together before securing the other end to the bar in the headboard. Within minutes, he's got another couple of longer lengths out, placing each one beside my hips. He pushes my right foot up to my bum, ties a knot around my ankle, then winds the length around my bent leg in a spiral upwards. Once he reaches my knee, he loops the rest of the rope back down again, capturing each coil of the spiral as he comes back down. The black lattice is so pretty against my pale skin, highlighting the tattoos I have there.

He does the other leg exactly the same, making me look a bit like a frog. It should be awkward, but it's actually very sexy. I am, however, already starting to ache. It's a good feeling, though. I also feel pride bubbling within me. I can take this. I can be good for him.

But holy shit, am I exposed. Vulnerable. Laid out like a feast, just waiting for Felix to devour me.

He places a large hand on my tummy and I realise I was wriggling, instinctively pulling against my restraints. "How do you feel, little one?"

I take a few deep breaths before nodding. "Good, Sir. It's completely weird, but I like it."

He bites his lip and looks at me with such adoration it's breathtaking. "I've been dreaming of getting my hands back on you all day," he says, his voice low and sensual. "We're going to play some games, Jack. I want you to feel everything as much as possible, so I'm going to blindfold you. I'll be with you every step of the way, okay? If anything gets too much, you use your safe word, and we'll pause."

"Yes, Sir," I say, keeping my voice firm. The idea of the blindfold freaks me out a bit, but I also know that I trust Felix, and he's right. If I don't like anything and need to stop, I know just one word will make him do that immediately.

But I don't want to use it.

"I can take it," I promise him. "Whatever you want to do to me, you can. I want to feel *everything.*"

He leans down and captures my mouth with his own, kissing me roughly. "Such a good boy," he mumbles against my lips. "All mine. I get to play with you just how I want. Let me hear all your pretty noises, good boy."

I whimper as he suddenly withdraws. I'm panting as I watch him reach behind the feather duster and reveal a silky black eye mask. My heart jumps in my chest, but I inhale and just breathe. He's right. If I can't see, I'll be able to focus that much better on all the touches he's going to give me.

He very carefully slips the mask over my face, putting it in just the right place. Then he rests his hand lightly on my chest, feeling the deep breaths I'm taking. After a few moments, however, they level out, and I feel a different kind of calm washing over me. The material isn't too tight over my eyes. I already feel kind of floaty and free, knowing that if I want to see again, that's up to Felix.

Everything is up to Felix now.

I realise I'm straining my ears, trying to hear what he's doing. But for such a large man, he's surprisingly silent as he moves around the room. I feel the bed dip and bounce a bit, but otherwise, I'm taken totally by surprise as the feather duster suddenly tickles my inner thigh.

I shriek and yank against my restraints. He laughs at me, but not in an unkind way. "You like that?"

I huff and laugh myself as he traces it up and down my leg, shivering at the way it affects my skin. "Yes, actually. Bastard."

He laughs louder at that, but then a kind of peace settles over the room as he works his way all over my body, making me squirm with the gentle touches. He even tickles my cock and balls, making me moan. I was half-hard, but it doesn't take much to get the blood flowing down there. I feel my length pulsing in time with the throbbing in my ears.

Just when I feel like it's maybe getting a bit too much, the feathers disappear. I grunt and lick my lips, resisting the urge to ask what's happening next. The whole point is not to know. Still, it's like I'm burning with anticipation, desperate for my next gift.

I gasp as something hard, cold, and slippery pushes against my hole. It's not a dildo, I don't think. It's too slim and rigid and...

Oh my god.

It's the handle of the feather duster, isn't it?

I laugh and moan at the same time, feeling ridiculous, like I'm cosplaying as an exotic bird. But I kind of love the idea that Felix is just stuffing me with whatever he wants. He pulses the handle inside me, not enough to touch my prostate, but enough to keep me aroused.

"You look so pretty," he rasps, and I snort.

"Trussed up like a turkey and filled with ostrich plumes," I grumble, but I'm sure he can see me smiling.

I still need to work on relaxing and letting go. It doesn't matter what I look like, only how I feel. That I'm submitting to Felix as my master. He knows what's best. He's going to take care of me and drive me wild. I just need to get out of my head and let him do it.

I'm not sure how long he has fun with the duster, but the next thing I know it's gone and in its place returns the familiar dildo. Actually, it might be an even bigger one? It burns as Felix eases it inside me despite how much lube it's coated in. But I have a feeling I know what he's doing.

He's training my hole. Stretching me out farther and farther so eventually I'll be ready to take his monster cock.

With that in mind, I accept the intrusion gratefully. I want him inside me so badly I could cry. In fact, I let out a sob in the here and now, letting my emotions rise to the surface as I sink deeper into subspace. I don't know how long I'll be able to call Felix mine. I want us to get to a point where there is nothing between us and we're as close as two people can possibly be.

He turns the vibration on and gets me mewling in moments. But then I hiss in shock as hot wax dribbles over my ribs. The heat is exhilarating, and as soon as the wax cools, I'm craving more.

He spills a few more times across my chest and belly, but then he covers one of my nipples, and I bite out a few curses at that, thrashing against my ropes.

"Shh, little one," he soothes me, kissing along my jaw. "It's okay. You can take it."

"Y-yes, Sir," I agree. It's unpleasant, but once it hardens, I like the way it pulls at my sensitive skin.

Not one to be predictable, the next sensation to assault me is freezing coldness on the other nipple, and I guess he got an ice cube from the Champagne bucket. He toys with my nipple for a few moments before bringing the cold wetness to my lips, rubbing the cube against them. I hadn't realised how dry my mouth had become, and I suck on it greedily.

"Good boy," he praises me, allowing me to drink it down until it melts through his fingers. I hear the rattle this time as he evidently reaches back into the bucket. But when he touches me again, the shocking chill slides right along my leaking cock.

I wail and try and get away, but there's nowhere to go. Felix hums as he drags the ice up and down my length, then over my balls. "These belong to me," he muses.

"Yes, yes," I cry, tears dampening my eye mask. I'm starting to approach the edge of what I think I can take. My body is on overload, and it knows that I'm perfectly trapped, completely at Felix's mercy.

I hear crunching and I wonder if Felix is eating the ice cube that he just ran all over my dick. That's kind of hot. Speaking of warmth, he makes up for tormenting me by wrapping his lips around my shaft and swallowing me down, the wet heat of his mouth blissful after the unpleasant coldness.

I thrust my hips up, but he's quick to push me back down, reminding me of who's in control. Instead, I whimper and gasp as he enthusiastically goes to town on my cock. But it doesn't last for long. Just as I'm starting to feel my climax building, he pops off, giving the tip a little parting kiss.

"Urgh, *Felix!*" I cry in frustration.

He laughs and moves up to nuzzle his nose against my cheek. "That's 'Sir' to you, remember, little thief?"

I make a keening noise. "Please," I whisper. "Please, Sir, please."

"It's okay, sweetheart," he says, pushing on the base of the dildo, pressing the vibrating tip against my prostate, and making me wail. "You're doing so well. Just hold on for me a little longer. I have one more game I want to play. It should help centre your mind. Then I'm going to make us come all over you."

I take a shaky breath and nod. Just one more thing and then he'll let me come. I can do that. And I know it's going to feel *so* good when I do. I need to be patient.

I'd forgotten about the small pinwheel until sharp pricks start travelling along the inside of my arm where it's tied above my head. I let out a low groan, my whole being zoning in on those consecutive little flashes of pain. Trembles come over my body in waves as he trails the device up and down my arms before starting on my chest. Sometimes he presses harder than others, making me hiss, but I'm absolutely loving it. I'm also wondering if it will leave any marks. I kind of hope so, even if just briefly. Like my flaming arse yesterday, I want to cling to some proof that this happened. That I took everything he gave me and begged for more.

That we were really together like this at all, and it wasn't all just some beautiful dream.

The bed dips again, and I can tell he's kneeling on either side of my hips. From the delicious squelching noises I can hear, I know he's wanking himself off whilst looking down at the mess he's made of me.

There he goes again, making me feel like the centre of the universe.

"Felix," I moan.

"Jack," he answers, already sounding wrecked. He's marked me all over, and now he's going to cover me with his seed like a wild animal. I shiver in anticipation, letting my mouth hang over in the hopes I might catch some on my lips and tongue.

It doesn't take him long to start roaring, and I feel the first creamy ropes hit my skin. He sprays my chest, face, and all over my straining cock. I feel utterly debauched as I swallow down the little saltiness I manage to capture, and in no time at all, he's using his own cum as lubricant to get me off.

Unsurprisingly, it takes about 0.5 seconds after the way he's teased me for what felt like an hour. I scream as I explode all over his hand, and my mess mixes with his that's already cooling on my body.

I'm properly sobbing into my eye mask as he slips it off and drops it onto the bed beside me. "That's right, gorgeous boy," he says, cupping the side of my face with his big hand. He rests my forehead against his and lets me cry it all out. "You were so good for me. Absolutely perfect. I need to free you now."

"Wait," I squeak. My vision is still a little blurred, so I blink and try extra hard to get his face into focus. "Can we stay like this just a bit longer?"

He purses his lips and looks me over. "Okay, little one. But only for a minute or two. I need to untie you and make sure you're not too achy."

I nod. "That's fine," I say. I just don't want to immediately rush from this moment. I want to savour it for a while.

He does turn off the vibrator, and I must admit that's a relief. Then he curls up his clothed body against my naked, marked, and bound one. My jailer is tender as he buries his face against my neck and gently trails his fingers over my abused skin. I inhale him into my lungs, committing him to the farthest depths of my memory.

The future is uncertain. But I know for sure that I'm going to remember this night for as long as I live.

CHAPTER 17

Felix

I HAVE PLENTY OF STUNNING WORKS OF ART IN MY HOME. BUT I'm not sure anything will ever compare now to the sight of Jack's beautiful naked body tied up on my bed, covered in our mixed cum, dried wax, rose petals, and trails of tiny bite marks from the pinwheel.

The caretaker in me wanted to release him immediately and tend to his every ache and pain. But the possessive man in me appreciated being allowed to hold him in that state for just a little while, simply because that was what he wanted. His trust in me was palpable.

Eventually, I do insist on untying and cleaning him up. I know I can't keep pushing him like this every night, but I'm just so bloody excited. I feel like I've woken up from years in a coma, and it's Jack who's taken me off life support.

I'm not young and foolish anymore, though. I have thought long and hard about whether or not this is specifically about Jack or if any attractive man could have stumbled into my lap and elicited the same reaction. And for a minute I considered that could be the case if that person were just the right kind of broken and scarred to match up my own fucked-up trauma. If they were gorgeous and tattooed and just the right amount of grumpy and bratty. If they were the perfect pocket size to compliment my massive form.

And I came to the conclusion that it was *absolutely* Jack himself who is responsible for my revival. This isn't just my dick getting excited by a hot man in my vicinity.

This is my heart completely falling head over heels for a particularly amazing man.

I allow Jack to doze a little after our endeavour. Then when he comes around naturally, I insist on rousing him into sitting upright and letting me feed him some proper food as well as hydrating him. The Champagne ended up going back into the fridge undrunk, but that's okay. We'll have another chance.

I let him sleep in this morning, as he clearly needed it. I, on the other hand, woke up full of beans with a hundred ideas going around my head. I surprised the hell out of my PA by calling her up and asking her to get the board of directors together for a meeting. I've left this ship drifting rudderless for too long.

The beautiful thing about Zoom is that unless someone's in surgery, I can pretty much demand that all my senior leadership drop whatever they're doing and log on. For the first time in years, I ask them for an update and actually properly pay attention to what they have to tell me.

Several of them seem flustered that this is some sort of surprise test on my part. It really isn't. I just want to make sure that I don't accidentally sell off entire branches again without even noticing. In fact, once they've managed to stammer their way through their rough reports, that's my first matter of business. I ask them to run me through exactly what the hell happened with the Dagenham department and the other half a dozen sites we sold on.

They try and tell me it's not my concern now we no

longer run those branches. I tell them it's very much my concern, and there is some frantic sifting through our database as well as online to get me my answers.

It transpires that Dagenham was the only one to be liquidated and the staff let go with barely any severance. I'm so ashamed of what I let happen to all those people, but now is not the time to dwell on that. Now we need to move forward.

"What's happened to the physical site?" I ask.

There's some clicking and wiggling of mice I hear through the screens. "It's just been left there for the time being," someone pipes up, their eyebrows raised. "It's due for demolition in January."

Relief rushes through me. "Excellent," I say into my camera with a big grin. "We're going to re-acquire it and offer every single terminated employee back their job."

There's a rather pregnant pause. "But, sir…" my CFO utters. "We can't…"

"According to the numbers you all just gave me," I say lightly, "if I forfeit my quite frankly ridiculous bonus in April, then that combined with a few other assets should mean we have more than enough capital to cover it."

Again, for a few seconds, nobody moves. "Sir, if I may speak openly," my CFO pipes up again. He's a shrewd man that I've never cared for, if I'm being blunt, but he's undoubtedly the reason why we're all so rich.

"Please do," I encourage him.

"If you reject your bonus, it sets, uh, an *uncomfortable* precedent for the rest of us."

I raise my eyebrows and blink. "Oh?" I say like I have no clue what he's talking about and *definitely* didn't plan this.

He shifts in his seat on the other side of the camera, and I catch a few other people doing the same thing. "If you give away your bonus, then…well…it would look bad if the other senior leadership didn't do the same."

I rub my chin. "Well, if that's the way it has to be just for this year, I guess the silver lining is that we'd be able to make all the improvements to this particular plant that led to its failing in the first place. And probably give all the employees raises. Right?"

I make that last word sound like a curious question, as if I haven't already run all the numbers three times over.

My CFO's mouth opens and closes a like a little goldfish. "That…could be possible, yes," he admits. "I'd need to run a few models and—"

"Excellent," I interrupt, clapping my hands. "I want the deal secured today. It was our property in the first place, so it shouldn't be too difficult. Contact the worker's union and let them know about the very hopeful employment prospects we intend to offer those workers in case they're in the process of accepting worse-paying jobs. It is right before Christmas, after all. We owe it to those people to try and give them the best chances. They're part of this company's family, yes?"

I see some very pale faces in the little boxes on my large screen. My PA gleefully unmutes herself. "Wonderful news, boss," she says loudly. "I'll contact the union with the update right away."

"Fantastic," I say with a nod. "Well, I think I can leave the rest of the details to you fine people. Please keep me in the loop."

I close my video feed, trusting that they will, and also that this time, I'll actually read whatever's sent to me and play an active part in where we go from what they have to say. I want to know where this company my family built from the ground up is thriving and, more importantly, where it's failing. I want to do better, achieve higher.

And truth be told, there's a voice lurking in the back of my mind whispering the idea that I've had for years but have been too chicken shit to act on.

If I can get the company healthy…I can maybe step down as CEO.

My father and grandfather would spin in their graves, I know. I'm sure my mother would think I'd lost my mind. But I think that after almost three decades, I can admit I've never felt any kind of passion for this industry, for leadership, for any of it.

I get my kicks from nurturing one on one. That's become startlingly clear again from this past week with Jack. I don't care about running an empire. I care about seeing someone's confidence blossom.

His confidence.

I want to help him discover his own joys and goals in life. I want to push him intimately and witness his beautiful submission to me. I want to lift him up to heights he couldn't imagine.

After all, I'm tall enough to do that literally.

But I've reached an age where I also understand patience. There's a part of me that's terrified because life can be far too short. However, experience has taught me that most things do not happen overnight.

A dream has taken hold of me now, though. I've got less than two years until I'm fifty. A lot can happen in two years. By then, I could have stepped away entirely from the company or at least moved down into a much more behind-the-scenes role. I've got enough money to last me a lifetime, after all.

I could be with someone I truly love, out and proud in the world as a gay man for the first time ever. I could take him on glamorous, exotic getaways or just stay snuggled up with him by the fire.

Maybe I'll trade this isolated floating castle for a real home. One with a garden amongst the trees. I'd love to live near a steam. Just...*be* in nature again, not cultivate it five hundred and fifty feet above the ground.

But the most important thing I'll have is hope. What is life without hope, anyway? I've forgotten what it's like to aspire, to reach, to fulfil.

And it's all because of one grumpy little thief who opened up my heart again without even meaning to.

"Take care, goodbye!" Goose squawks, reminding me that the meeting is over. He flies around the room before landing on my shoulder.

I've always locked him out in the past when I've taken video conferences. But today I really didn't see why I should. After his initial outburst about tea and crumpets, the queen, and a few choice words about the weather, there were several shocked stares. But by the end of our time together, people were openly laughing at my silly Goose.

No, not people. My team.

There was a time when I used to send out Christmas cards out to all the branch managers and know their partners' names. When I was aware of exactly how hard they'd worked to oversee their bonuses (which I pinky promise everyone else will get and the senior execs will get next financial year). But I've delegated that shit for years.

No more.

I'm elbow-deep in ordering hampers to be delivered for the festive season when my study door creaks, and I look up to see a rumpled Jack peeking around the door.

"Hello, sweetheart," I say in delight, then glance at my watch in horror. It's almost eleven. "Oh, fuck! I'm so sorry. I was going to make you breakfast, but I got caught up. How about brunch instead? Oh, did you take your meds?"

He gives me such an adorable smile. "You left them by my

side of the bed," he says in a small voice. Like he's worried if he's too loud it won't be true anymore.

I get up from my desk and walk around it in a matter of steps so I can wrap him up in my arms. "Of course, little one. You were probably a bit distracted last night, but I moved all your stuff in there yesterday. Your clothes, toiletries, all of it."

He bites his lip and looks up at me. "You did?"

I arch an eyebrow. "Should I have asked first?"

I promised myself I wouldn't smother him or move too fast, but then I go and do that. I'm an idiot. But it was his meds that made me think of it in the first place. I didn't want him to have to trek it downstairs in order to take one pill when he woke up. Then it just seemed logical to pick everything else up at the same time.

He scoffs and frowns at me. "Since when do you ask for permission?" he grumbles. Only he could make a scathing remark sound like a loving compliment. "I just...don't want to get in your way."

I sigh and drag him over to my sofa, where we made out yesterday, and sit down. "You're too tiny to ever get in my way, little one," I say with a grin. He scowls and smacks my arm, making me drop my head back and laugh. "Seriously, you're right. This is my home, and I do what I want. What makes me happy. And what makes me happy is having you next to me, especially when I wake up. Besides, you're much easier to keep an eye on like that, my prisoner."

He rolls his eyes, but he snuggles in closer to me. However, doubt flickers through me. I keep meaning to tell him he can leave whenever he wants. That he's a free agent and I want him here because that's what *he* wants.

But I haven't.

Because I'm scared.

I was so powerless when I lost Henry. I appreciate it's given me control issues ever since. But if I'm bossing Jack around and he seems happy, it just feels so much easier to not say the words. To keep him here because I ordered him because I know that's what we both want.

He should have his freedom, though. I know that. This is all part of the fantasy bubble we've created for ourselves here. I'm sure that my feelings for him aren't some kind of whirlwind infatuation. I want to commit to a real, long-term relationship. But somewhere in the back of my mind is still that terrified eighteen-year-old who had to watch his first love slip away right before his eyes. I want to fight for Jack.

But he has to fight for it as well.

"Busy morning, then?" Jack asks, pulling me from my thoughts.

I shake myself mentally and smile. We can cross all those bridges when we come to them. Right now, I'm still riding the high of resurrecting myself for my company and talking with so many human beings in just one morning. Sure, they were all little faces on videos, but I still got a lot of energy from them.

"Yes, actually," I say happily. "I'm finally pulling my head out of my arse and remembering that I own and run a company. I called a spontaneous board meeting and feel like I've got my foot back on the pedal again. I've been looking over quarterly reports and buying Christmas presents for my cleaners' families. It feels…good." I nod and beam at him. "Like I've come out of hibernation. I'm done acting like a zombie. Oh, and your mum won't have to worry anymore! We're sorting out the Dagenham branch as we speak. She'll have her job back in no time. Or better, if I can manage it!"

I'm used to Jack being a little raincloud or looking at me with scepticism. But his expression right now is more diffi-cult to read. He's smiling, but it's tight, and his eyes are somewhat fixed. "That's great," he says in a perfectly pleasant tone, but something still isn't quite sitting right with me. I think I've missed something. I thought he'd be over the moon.

"I'm sorry I missed making you breakfast because I got wrapped up," I say, genuinely starting to fret. But he's already shaking his head vehemently.

"Don't be ridiculous. You have to work. You don't have to dote on me every waking moment. I'm fine."

He's still smiling, but I'm not totally convinced.

Well, part of the problem is I fucked his brains out last night then only got him to nibble through half a sandwich afterwards. He needs a proper meal, then we can talk about things. Not that I'm sure what there is to talk about, but something isn't quite right.

I try not to worry.

I'm certain after a lot of carbs and perhaps some more snuggling, everything will be fine.

Nothing to worry about.

Right?

CHAPTER 18

Jack

So that's it, then.

It's over.

I force myself to smile and ghost my way through the day. I'm happy that Felix is moving on with his life. I *am*. He deserves that much. I'm just also allowed to be fucking devastated because I know that doesn't include a place for me.

I mean, come on? Some scrawny little inexperienced thief who smashed his way into a billionaire's life? It's utterly ridiculous. I don't belong here.

Not for long, anyway.

Right now, I can cling to *something*. I can eke out the last little bit of bliss from this time I've borrowed up here in the clouds. I can be proud of my accomplishments in all the forms they've presented themselves, and I can walk away a far better man than the one I crept in here as.

My focus is singular as I work non-stop for hours getting the last of Felix's precious coins back into their individually sized indents. I even bring my lunch into the safe, as I don't think I can cheerfully sit opposite Felix and make small talk whilst my heart is silently breaking into more tiny pieces than the glass display top I shattered in here mere days ago.

I'm being pathetic. It *has* only been days. This thing between us is just an infatuation. A product of extraordinary circumstances. It only feels so intense because I'm still in the thick of it. Once I get back to my real life and find some room to breathe, it won't feel so all-consuming anymore.

At least, I hope it won't. Because I don't know how I'll survive otherwise, knowing that Felix is up here in the clouds, living his extraordinary life in a place where I'll never be able to see or touch him again.

This isn't my world, though, and I should be grateful for what little time I did get to spend here. Felix has given me experiences that I'll never forget for as long as I live. Shown me things about myself that I never knew before. He's a beautiful, generous man and I'll always be impossibly thankful that our paths crossed at all.

But I'm also greedy. Hello, thief? I need more, just a little more, before I let this dream go for good.

I brush my hands together and survey my finished project, feeling not a small amount of pride. The replacement glass cover is going to be delivered in a few days, but as of a few minutes ago, every single antique coin has safely been placed back in its original home. The rest of the contents in the safe are also neatly placed where they belong. It's not often that I feel like I truly achieve much in life, but this is something I can look back on with pride.

For the first time in days, I wish I had my phone so I can take a photo. Maybe I can once Felix gives it back before I leave. But I have a hunch the moment will have passed by then. Instead, I stand there a little longer, committing the sight to memory. I doubt it will comfort me much once I'm out of Felix's orbit forever, but I'm determined not to completely ruin this last evening for myself. I take a deep breath and try and channel a little of my lover's relentless positivity.

Some things aren't meant to stay long with us in this life. Sometimes people only come to us for a short amount of time, and that's just the way it's meant to be. I think of my dad. I think of Henry. It doesn't diminish our love for them because they were taken from us too soon.

I wonder if I love Felix. I've certainly never felt like this about anyone before in my life, so perhaps. I don't have anything to compare it to. I just know that when he's near me, I feel whole.

When I leave, I'll have to remember how to live with being broken again.

I shake myself. This isn't what I want. My work is done, so it's time to celebrate. I reach deep within myself and look for the spark of joy I know is there, even if it's hiding. Felix has taught me that much. Life is too short and too hard to always be looking for the negatives. Not everyone is trying to screw each other over all the time. It's okay to be vulnerable on occasion and let other people in.

I really want to let Felix in.

Inhaling long and slow, I turn away and step out of the safe for the last time, once more grateful that Felix is as kind as he is. I should be in jail—*again*—but I'm not. That alone should be enough to make me thankful.

I just wish Felix wasn't so completely out of my league. But it's pointless trying to change the facts. He's getting back to his real life as the CEO of a multi-billion-pound company and if he's telling the truth—if Mum can really get her job back—then all I need to worry about now is getting myself something fast so I don't go under after all of this. Lots of places should be hiring seasonal staff and hopefully they won't be put off by my stint in prison, so I'll probably be okay.

This was a nice dalliance. The best, actually. One of the most incredible experiences of my life.

But it's over now. I need to make peace with saying goodbye.

I'm allowing myself one little selfish indulgence, though. If I get my way, that goodbye will last all night.

I find Felix in his office once again, his face creased with concentration as he types away on his keyboard. Goose is asleep on his perch in the corner. Neither of them notices me slip into the room. Not until I'm practically in Felix's lap, anyway. Then he snaps his attention to me quick enough.

Urgh. His face splits into the most magnificent smile. "Hello, sweetheart," he says, sounding genuinely thrilled to see me. "How are you doing?"

I force myself to smile too as he pulls me between his knees, his enormous hands resting on my hips. I slip my hands around the back of his neck. "It's done," I say with sincere pride. "It's all repaired."

His eyebrows shoot up. "The coins?" I nod. "That's awesome!" He laughs and hugs me to him. "Well done, gorgeous. Thank you. That means so much to me. I'll think of you every time I look at it now."

I hope that's true. I'd like to hope that even though I'll be gone, a little part of me might linger, at least for a while. I don't want to disappear from Felix's life as quickly as I fell into it.

"Are you done for the day?" I ask, echoing his question from yesterday when he picked me up to go fuck my brains out.

He gives me that cheeky, lopsided smile and clicks something on his computer, making the screen go dark. "I am now."

I step away, intertwining our hands so I can pull him along with me. "Come to bed," I say softly.

He must sense something about my mood because he doesn't tease or play with me. He just rises to his feet, his gaze smouldering as he watches me walk backwards until I turn around and lead him from the room. His hand is so big and sturdy in mine.

I wish I could hold on to it forever.

Tonight will have to do.

He carefully rubs his thumb over the cut on my palm from the glass that's healing nicely. I stopped wearing a plaster a while ago, and now it's just a pink line. A part of me wishes it would scar so I could keep it long after I leave here, but I doubt it will.

He quietly follows me into his room, letting me tug him towards the bed. "Be with me," I murmur.

He stops so we're both standing by the edge, and he cups both sides of my face. "I'm right here, little one."

I nod, doing my best not to get choked up. I desperately don't want to spoil this for us. "I don't want to play or call you 'Sir'. Can you make love to me, Felix?"

He leans down and captures my mouth. The kiss is sensual and full of promises I know he won't get the chance to keep. I shove my heartache down, losing myself in the taste of his lips and the feel of his strong hands on my body.

"Anything for you, Jack," he says. I believe him.

He slips his fingers under my T-shirt, tickling my stomach with his caress before pulling it over my head. I undo his belt, pulling it through the loops of his trousers and dropping it on the floor. I pop the buttons on his fly one by one, then skim my fingers over the enormous bulge in his briefs.

"I want you inside me," I say, looking into his eyes, showing him that I really mean it. "I'm ready. I can take it."

He licks his lips and nods. "I want that as well, sweetheart. And…and I don't want to use any condoms."

I blink and stare at him for a second. I can see he's nervous, but his gaze doesn't flinch away from mine. "Felix, you know that I—"

"That you're untransmittable, yes," he says firmly.

"Yes," I agree, but I'm uncertain. Henry's death has traumatised him for decades. This isn't a decision I want him to make lightly. "But I don't mind—"

"I do," he interrupts again. "I don't want anything between us. It's okay if you don't want to do anything kinky tonight, but I'm going to still get my Dom side out for this. If you want me to wear protection for your sake, that's different. Of course I will. But if you're trying to anticipate any reservations on my part, don't. I know what I want, and that's you, Jack Spriggs. All of you. I trust you not to hurt me."

I swallow. That's exactly what I came to do when I broke in here several days ago. Now I would do anything to avoid bringing him harm.

I run my hands up and down his sides, then rest them on his chest, looking into his blue eyes. "I want all of you as well, Felix Fagiolo." What of him I can get, in any case. I take comfort knowing that I can borrow him for a little while longer at least.

"Okay, then," he says, sounding relieved. "Decision made."

We continue to gently undress each other until we're completely naked. His big, hairy body is like a vista stretching out into the distance. I want to explore every inch of it.

He pulls the covers back and drags me into bed, wrapping his long, thick limbs around my body, cocooning me as he kisses me deeply and sensually. I'm vibrating all over, my cock already half-hard and sensitive to his every touch. We're side by side with his leg slung over mine and his hands gripping my hip and tugging my hair.

After a little while, he pulls back from kissing my mouth,

instead rubbing his middle and index fingers against my swollen lips before easing them into my mouth. Obediently, I suck, loving the way his pupils dilate as he watches me.

God, even if I had forever to explore with this man in bed, I don't think it would be enough. I could suck his giant cock every day, let him use my body in a million different ways to pleasure himself, be held by him and loved by him…

I let those thoughts drift away. That life isn't possible, but right now is. I need to remember every single second of it and not get lost in 'what-ifs'.

Once his digits are slick with my spit, he moves around then hoicks my leg up over his hip, exposing my hole so he can rub his wet fingers against it. I bury my face against his neck, but he hums in displeasure.

"Please look at me, Jack," he says, his voice low and sensual, pleading almost.

I know he probably can't help himself by still being a little controlling, but it's okay. This is a level I'm comfortable with for tonight. It's how he's showing me he cares about me and that he knows what's best for the both of us.

I take a breath and pull my head back so our gazes are connected again. He beams at me as he gently strokes my slippery hole. "That's it, sweetheart. I want you right here with me the whole time, okay?"

I nod. "Yes, okay. I want that, too."

"Good boy."

He kisses my mouth some more as he teases my entrance. But when it's time to breach me, he breaks away so he can reach for the lube, making things even easier. After the past few days, his two fingers push through my tight ring of muscle with little resistance. I moan all the same, especially when he brushes against my prostate.

I rut against him, finding friction for both of our cocks between our bellies. He soon adds a third finger inside me, and it burns, but I can take it without much fuss. I'm hungry for the main event, breathless with want and desire.

"Can I ride you?" I mumble against his lips.

He blinks and caresses the short hairs at the back of my neck. "You can have whatever you want, little one. I'm yours."

I wish that were true, but I like to think he means it in this moment. I'm his in all the ways that matter the most tonight.

He rolls onto his back and picks up the lube again, coating his cock with it. I love just watching him stroke himself, the huge member sliding in and out of his fist. But then it's my turn, and finally, *finally*, I get to climb him the way I dreamed of when I very first laid eyes on him.

He holds the base of his shaft as I angle myself on top of him, docking his tip into my hole and gradually starting to lower myself down onto it. I gasp as he rubs my sides, making soothing noises.

"That's it, sweetheart," he assures me. "Take it slow. You feel fucking incredible. You're doing so well."

I grunt and grit my teeth, sweat pouring down my body. The air stinks of masculine musk, and I drink it into my lungs. It feels like an impossibility, but the burn does begin to ease as my body stretches to accommodate Felix deep inside me. I cling to his chest, digging my fingers into his flesh. He marked me the previous night, and now I want to mark him back.

My thighs are trembling by the time I sink down as far as I can go. I've never felt so full in my life, and I breathe deeply, giving myself time to adjust. Felix rubs up and down my arms, leaning up to kiss my lips, my cheek, along my jaw, and down my neck.

"You look *stunning*," he rasps, holding onto my hips. "And you feel even better."

He grins wickedly, and I can't help but laugh. "You feel

pretty good, too," I admit. It's a lot, but the pressure is easing by the second. He gives an experimental roll of his hips, and I groan and let my eyes flutter closed. "Wow."

He thrusts up gently again and I push down, finding a rhythm. Holy fuck, it's like nothing else I've ever experienced before. My toes curl, and I make a keening noise as he starts to pick up the pace. I feel like he's fucking my tonsils, and I choke for air.

We rock together, thrusting the bed against the wall as we growl and grunt and pant like animals. It's taking everything I have to bear down and fight against his raw power, but I'm desperate for him, for this, for us, so it makes every exhausting second worth it.

I'm already seeing stars when he wraps his massive hand around my hard and leaking cock. I scream and scratch my nails down his chest, leaving red welts in their wake.

"Come for me, Jack," he utters. "Come all over me. Come now."

Everything shatters as I let go, spilling my load across his hand and chest. I'm flying free and the tears cascade down my face. He's still slamming into me, chasing his own climax as I unravel, when suddenly he arches his back, and I feel him pulsing inside me as he gnashes his teeth and howls.

As he flops back against the bed, he throws his arms around my back and hauls me down on top of him, crushing us together as he buries his face against my neck. "Baby," he breathes softly.

I bite my lip and screw up my eyes, unable to stop the tears from flowing as my emotions overwhelm me.

I don't want to go.

But it's time.

CHAPTER 19
Felix

WHEN I WAKE THE NEXT MORNING, JACK IS GONE.

I remind myself that it's a big apartment and he can go wherever he likes. But something isn't sitting right in my chest, so I extract myself from the rumpled bed, pull on some jogging bottoms, and head out to find him.

The penthouse is too still.

"Jack?" I call out.

"Jack! Jack!" Goose repeats back at me. He flies through the air to land on my shoulder and nuzzles his face against my cheek.

I gently stroke the fine hair-like feathers on the back of his neck. "Good boy," I murmur, but my attention is focused on scanning over the balcony. I can't see Jack in the main living area. He's probably just in the shower or something, but the nagging worry at the back of my mind won't leave me alone. "Jack?" I call out again as I jog down the stairs.

I quickly poke my head into the spare room that he slept in the first few nights but it's as empty as when I cleared it out. He might be on the terrace, I realise. But I decide to check downstairs first just in case, as I'm closer to there now.

I've more or less convinced myself that he's sat outside, enjoying the morning. That's why I can't sense him around. I'll bring a blanket up with me as he might not have realised how cold it can get this time of year, even though the sun is shining. He might have made himself tea, but I have the wild urge to make him hot chocolate and bacon sandwiches.

I know why I'm on edge. Last night something wasn't quite right. He seemed melancholy. Desperate. We made love, and it was beautiful, but this morning we need to talk. I have to know what's troubling him so I can make it better. Until I can discover what that is, food will have to do.

Except he's not on the terrace.

He's sat fully dressed in front of the open safe door at the chair and little table I was using whenever I helped him out. His backpack is by his feet. I realise he's not wearing my clothes but the ones he arrived in.

Between his fingers on the small table is an empty sheet of pills, the perforated foil on the back catching in the light as he twists it around.

My stomach drops. "Jack?" I croak, dread pooling inside me.

His eyes flick upwards. They're puffy. It's clear he's been crying. He licks his lips and tries to muster a smile for me. "Hey, Felix," he says heavily.

I fly to his side and drop to my knees, resting my hand on his leg and looking up at him imploringly. Goose darts away, going to go sit quietly on his perch for a change. "Jack, what's wrong? You're scaring me. Did I do something to upset you?"

His laugh is hollow as he shakes his head. "God, no. Isn't that funny? That's the whole reason I came here. I was so violently hurt. But it wasn't even you at all in the end."

I frown, a lump forming in my throat as I try and battle down my confusion. "Talk to me, sweetheart. What's wrong?"

He shakes his head again and holds up the pill packet. "Nothing," he says softly. "It's just time."

"Time for what?" I ask, baffled.

"Time for me to go."

For several long seconds, I just stare at him, not understanding. "Go where?" I ask eventually.

"I'm out of meds," he says, placing the empty sheet down on the table and leaving it there. "I've finished fixing the damage I caused. I need to go. Get back to my real life."

I'm not following. I guess he wants to pick up more meds. But we could also order more to be delivered here as well. Why is he so sad?

"Okay," I say slowly. "That's fine, baby. You've been cooped up here for almost a week. I wanted to talk to you about this anyway. About giving you your phone back and talking about how this is going to work. You probably want to see your mum and..." And *why* does he still look devastated? "When are you coming back?"

He takes a shaky breath. "No, Felix." He sounds like he's taking pity on me.

"Jack," I say firmly. "I don't understand. Please talk to me. What's going on in your head? What does 'no' mean?"

"No, I'm not coming back," he says softly, tears brimming in his eyes.

My heart drops, and I reach to grasp his hands in mine. "Why on earth not?" I splutter.

He screws up his eyes for a second, squeezing out tears and making his cheeks damp. "Because this isn't real, is it? It's been a fun game, playing as your prisoner. But you've got your own actual life to get back to, and I don't fit into it."

I'm so stunned it takes me a few seconds to flounder around for the right words, any words. "Bull*shit* you don't fit into my life," I exclaim. "No one has ever fit *more* perfectly! Jack, you clearly don't want to leave, and I don't want you to leave, so why don't we just calm down and talk it through."

He lets out a frustrated snarl and yanks his hands away before getting to his feet. I also stand, staring at him in disbelief. "This relentless positivity of yours gives you blinkers, Felix! This is insane! You're a literal billionaire, and I'm the scrappy fuck who broke into your house to try and *rob* you! In what reality are we a good match? I don't belong here. It was a fun game but now I have to go. Please give me back my phone."

I'm breathing hard as I stare at him. Yes, I know I always try and look on the bright side and am determined to find solutions to every problem I encounter—usually by throwing money at them, admittedly—but he's going to find out how angry he's making me pretty bloody quickly.

"This was just a game to you?" I ask quietly.

Bollocks to that. I've seen every emotion that played across his face, and this was equally as intense and moving for him as it was for me.

He's afraid.

That I can understand, but only if he doesn't walk out on me right now.

"It meant everything to me," Jack bites back. "But it's not sustainable. It was a holiday! And holidays end. I'm not hanging around until you get bored of playing with me. I have to get back to my life and start to try and repair that now. My mum depends on me. I can't just leave her all alone."

This is my fault. I should have given him back his phone the second we cleared things up and became friends. Became lovers. I was too afraid myself, and instead of telling him he could go whenever he wanted, I made him think he was still trapped here.

I was so scared of losing him that I've pushed him into walking away for good.

"No, no," I say, squeezing my head in my hands. "Jack, I want you to be free. I want you to take care of your mum. Hell, *I* want to take care of your mum! We can do all that. Why would you walk away from me? Why does this have to be the end?"

"Because I can't have all this!" he explodes. "I'm a bad person! I can't wake up in a fairy tale and expect to keep it all. It's not fair or right. And I'm not sticking around for it all to turn sour. No one ever wants to stay with me. I'm toxic! I literally spent time in *jail*. Your company might not care if you come out as gay, but they're sure as hell going to have a problem with that, I'm sure. So I'll leave now before you can grow to resent me."

His revelation about prison doesn't surprise me. I suspected as much. I'm too busy being shocked by everything else he's saying, if I'm honest.

"I'm feeling pretty resentful right now," I snap. God, I feel like my heart has been slashed open. The first man I've fallen for since I lost Henry, and he's saying this was all just some dalliance for him? "I was always honest with you, Jack. *Always.* And maybe there were conversations we should have had before, because obviously you're filling in the blanks and just making shit up! Every relationship has the potential to end badly. But if you don't even try, then how will you ever find happiness?"

He scoffs and scrubs his face. "You've been hiding up here too long," he says miserably. "I just fell into your lap. If you're going to start getting back into the real world, you'll realise there are far better guys out there than me. Nicer, more suitable men. Ones without criminal records."

"I don't want some hypothetical man!" I yell. "I want you! You're being ridiculous—"

"Don't tell me what I am!" he cries, fighting back more tears. "I know I'm beneath you in every way. It was fun being your pet for a while, but I can't stay here in your massive penthouse with your billions of pounds. I *can't.* It'll kill me when it all comes falling down. It's just Stockholm syndrome. It's not real. Now please give me my phone."

I just stand there for a few seconds, the numbness creeping in. "I'll fight for you, Jack," I say hollowly. "I'll fight so hard to make you see you're everything I want and more. But if you're telling me that you *don't* want this…don't want me…I'll let you go. You have to say it, though. If you really want to leave…of course you're free to go."

He swallows, our eyes locked on one another.

And then he looks away.

"I don't want this," he whispers.

It's as if the tiny seedling that was flourishing in my heart withers and dies in an instant. I've been a fool. I know my feelings for him were real, but maybe he was conning me the whole time? I don't want to believe it, but I'm desperately struggling to try and explain his complete turnaround this morning.

Last night was so beautiful. Now he's throwing it all back in my face.

If he truly doesn't want this—to work out what a real relationship would look like between us—then I can't force him. We're both afraid, but he's a coward if he's going to give up on it all now, and there's nothing I can do to change his mind.

He needs to love himself before he can love someone else. That much is clear.

I feel like a zombie as I walk to the kitchen and fetch his phone. It's just been sitting there in a drawer after I charged it back up to full battery. I shuffle over to where he's determinedly staring at the floor, and hold it out.

"Thank you," he mumbles as he pulls it from my grasp and pockets it. He still doesn't look at me as he picks up his backpack and shrugs it on. "Thank you for everything. I really am sorry."

Something cracks inside me as I watch him walk towards the front door. "You know, you never really were a prisoner here, Jack," I say softly and jut my head towards the door. He frowns and glances at me briefly before he reaches for the handle.

The door opens.

I unlocked it that very first day. He just never bothered to try it again.

Because he wanted to be here. I know he did.

Not anymore, though.

He stares out into the lobby for a moment, then takes a deep breath. "Goodbye, Felix. I'll never forget you," he says without looking back at me.

And then he's gone.

I watch the door closing behind him and stare at it for god knows how long. I'd forgotten how much pain one human being could inflict on another person, even if it was unintentional.

This is why I've stayed away for years. This is why I let myself go numb. Because I can't stand this kind of torture. I never could.

It's worse because I don't understand. I truly don't. I thought we were connecting, that we were so amazing together. But was he just going through the motions to get out of being arrested?

Perhaps.

The only thing I know is that he doesn't want me. That he's walked away. So that's it. I have to accept it.

All that hope that has been blossoming from within me

the past several days evaporates in an instant. Suddenly, I don't remember what I'm living for all over again.

It's going to take much, much longer to repair this than it did the damage in the safe.

Much longer.

CHAPTER 20

Jack

I never knew I could feel such pain.

It's different to when I lost my dad. That was horrific. I raged and hurtled my anger into the world, blazing fire wherever I went.

This is a horrible, freezing emptiness that I've inflicted on myself.

I rub my hand against my eyes again, bumbling my way along the street. I got the tube out of central London, but I got off a stop early so I could walk for a while and try and clear my head.

I really hate myself right now. But I can't let go of the cold, hard facts that my time in the penthouse was just a fantasy. Felix was finally coming out of himself and returning to the real world. He has a company to run, and once he remembers all the fancy things he used to do, the important people he knows, and the expensive parties he should be attending, I won't fit in at all. In fact, I'll be horribly out of place, and leaving then would be much, much worse.

Not that I can imagine anything worse than right now. But it will fade with time. That, I have to trust.

No, I've done the right thing, I'm sure. Life isn't a fairy tale. People like me don't just hit the jackpot over night. I was lucky to have the days I did with Felix. Now it's time to move on.

I can't stand to imagine the humiliation for us both if people in his circles ever discovered I was a criminal that had done time. He's practically aristocracy. The scandal it would cause doesn't bear thinking about. I know I broke his heart just now by leaving. The hurt I saw on his face with haunt me forever. But it's better to do that now rather than destroy his reputation and make *him* have to be the bad guy when he inevitably dumps me later down the line.

I take a shaky breath and shove my hands farther into my jacket pockets. It's nowhere near as warm as my dad's old leather jacket, but that's just another thing I'm going to have to come to terms with. Who knows when Micky will give that back? If he ever will. That pain is sharp and cuts through my chest like a knife.

For a second, anger flashes through me at Felix. Why did he have to be there? Knowing what I do about him now, it's no surprise that he cancelled his New York trip on a whim. But if he hadn't been there like I'd planned, then I'd have gotten my payday. I'd have my leather jacket back, and…

And I never would have met Felix.

I almost lose it again at that thought. Despite this agony, I can't bring myself to wish for that. Our time together was precious, even if it was short. I think our paths were meant to cross. We just weren't meant to walk together.

I curse myself for all the poor life choices I've made, fantasising for a moment that if I'd never gone to jail and fucked up my employment prospects, I'd probably be a lot more respectable. Not rich, but maybe someone who Felix wouldn't be ashamed to be associated with.

But then I keep coming back to the fact that we really would have never, ever met. Our circles would still be miles apart, and the prospect of a relationship between us would be almost just as ridiculous.

No. There's no alternate universe where I could…what? Be his boyfriend? Even just thinking the word makes me cringe. He's the kind of guy who deserves some minor royalty as a fiancé or something. Not some scruffy urchin practically from the pages of a Dickensian novel.

At least I can be there for my mum. As I turn down onto her street, I take a deep breath, pulling the cold air into my lungs. When I turned my phone back on, it was unsurprising that I had over a dozen messages from her, not to mention from Micky and other people. That's what happens when you fall off the grid and immediately cut all lines of communication. People worry. People care.

It still seems weird to me. But it's hard to deny all those notifications.

I shake it off, mentally and physically. I don't have the capacity to think about all these heavy thoughts at once. All I can think about is getting to my mum. I shot her a message asking if she was in and only waited to see her reply that she was. I ignored all her follow-up questions and just got straight on the underground. No doubt she's going to make me tell her everything now, and I don't want to waste time typing it all out.

I really don't want the story of my time with Felix just sitting on my phone, there for me to scroll up and relive any time I feel like hurting myself.

The old, terraced house is both incredibly familiar after the years I spent living here—and the years Mum's stayed here and I visited—but it all feels like a complete world away after my week in the clouds. This is why a relationship with Felix wasn't possible. We're literally from different planets. He could never understand what it's like to have to choose between heating or food in the winter. Just as I know I'd never feel comfortable living the life of luxury for long. It was fun for a vacation from reality, but I could never belong there, not in a million years.

The rusty gate squeaks as I open it. The grass is getting overgrown in the tiny front garden again. That's my fault. Mum can't mow it anymore, and I should have popped round a few weeks ago. I was just so consumed with my revenge plan that ultimately turned into nothing. I've let her down in so many ways, but now's the time I can make up for it.

I wonder if Felix was serious about getting Mum her job back. He didn't elaborate, and I should have pressed him for more details before I left. So now I'm still unsure about what I should do so she can pay rent next month. Perhaps the best course of action will be to act as if nothing has changed. Felix might not be interested in doing me any favours now anyway.

I'm worried I've fucked her over a second time, but as I rub my chest, I know that I couldn't have stayed just to ensure her employment. That would be icky. If I'd stayed, it would have been because I wanted to. Because I *could*. Not to earn favours. What we had was so much more than that, even if it was short.

Seasonal jobs don't pay well, though. She's been in this house for over fifteen years, but I don't doubt the landlord would seize any chance he could to kick her out and raise the prices for the next tenant. I guess I could move out of my place, and we could pool our resources together, but I don't really see how that's going to help when neither of us has a job right now. Cash-in-hand jobs are fine, but it doesn't exactly leave me with a lot of glowing references when trying to prove I can afford rent.

Because the truth is right now I can't.

I think of Felix's offer to pay off Micky and pause at the front door, my hand raised in front of the buzzer. He said he had money to burn. He'd probably try and sort both me and my mum out if I let him.

I *hate* myself that I want to accept it.

It was hard enough walking away from him this morning. But the idea of taking payment from him like a prostitute turns my stomach sour. I don't have anything against sex work at all, but that wasn't what we shared. What we had was precious, and I refuse to cheapen and sully it by making it transactional. That goes against everything I stand for. I'd rather rob a bank. It's just money—it would be insured, and no one would get hurt.

I don't ever want to hurt Felix more than I already have.

Recalling the look on his face as I told him I was going earlier makes the acid curling inside me boil. I know he wanted to be the sunshine and see the best in everything, as always, but I had to be the cold, hard realist. He's just infatuated with the first man to come his way in years. That's all it was. His loneliness.

And I couldn't stick around to watch him realise that. Leaving then would have ended me.

I shiver and close my hand into a fist. I need to ring the bell, but—

The door flies open.

"Are you just going to stand there all day? Jack William Spriggs, what on *Earth* is going on with you?"

I smile sheepishly as my mother throws her arms around me in a crushing hug. "Hi, Mum," I say weakly.

"Don't you 'hi, Mum' me," she scolds. "You get inside this house and start talking, understood?"

I chuckle and let her bundle me over the threshold. "Understood," I tell her. "But there better be tea."

"Tea *and* crumpets," she says smugly. "I'm not above bribery and blackmail, you know."

And she wonders where I get it from.

———

"So you just...left?"

Four crumpets and two cups of tea later, I've finished telling my mother a heavily edited version of events. I said I'd gone to Felix's place to assist on a plumbing job as I have genuinely helped install some bathrooms in my time. I implied that we'd hit it off and I'd volunteered to stay and take a look at some leaky taps and then one thing had led to another.

For several days.

Obviously, I *don't* have the money to show from this fictional job, but that's a problem for another time.

"Mum, he's rich," I try and explain. "Like, mega-rich. And I was the, um, plumber. It was just a bit of fun, but it was clear it wasn't going to last."

"And he said that, did he?"

She arches an eyebrow. Even in an old hoodie with her greying hair pulled up in a bun I still think she looks lovely. But she doesn't half know how to cut a stare. Her hands might be all twisted and achy, but her mind works just fine. I don't think she's all too fooled by my redacted account of the past week, but she's also smart enough not to call me out directly. I bet she's filling in some of the blanks on her own, however.

I open and close my mouth. "Not...technically."

"Jack," she bemoans, but I'm already shaking my head.

"He's a hopeless optimist, and it's a long time since he's

been in a relationship. He wanted to jump into something that was never going to last! One of us had to be realistic."

She sighs and gives me a withering look before patting my hand. "Life has been a bit hard on you, hun. And you're a natural pessimist, like me. Your dad was the cheerful one, god rest his soul. But I know you're not a bloody idiot."

"Umm?" I say. "I hope not?"

"Then why on Earth did you run away from the rich, handsome man who begged you to stay?"

I wince. I didn't even tell her half of how much he begged, but she sussed it out anyway. My heart aches in my chest as I think of his betrayed expression.

"It never would have worked, Mum," I whisper. I do my best to keep the tears at bay, but my eyes burn anyway. "We're from different worlds. I was just a plaything to him. It was fun, but that's not how relationships work."

She arches an eyebrow. "Can I say something that's probably going to make you cross?"

I sigh. "Go on, then."

She smacks my hand hard, making me hiss and yank it back to cradle it against my chest where she can't reach it. "You've never *had* a real relationship, have you? Unless there's been a secret boyfriend you were too ashamed to bring home?"

It's my turn to scowl. "I've had plenty of boyfriends," I grumble, not willing to admit that cum buddies don't equal actual dating.

"None that you had a real commitment with, though, hmm? *I* think..." She bites her lip and balls her fists, looking like she's ready to fight. Then it all comes out in one continuous breath. *"I think you were so devastated by your dad dying that you ran away from any nice guy that came your way and threw yourself at fuck bois instead."*

She grabs her mug of tea and peers at me over the rim.

My jaw drops open. "That's not...I don't..." My shoulders sag. "Fine. You might have a teeny, tiny point. But that doesn't change the fact that he's way out of my league, and I did us both a favour by finally leaving."

"Tell that to your face," she says with a grimace. "Hun, look. It's not too late, right? You go back over there tonight with flowers and chocolates and stuff and tell him you're an idiot who got scared. I mean...if that's what you want?"

I swallow around the lump that's risen in my throat. Felix asked me what I wanted.

I lied.

I lied so he'd let me go. I told him I didn't want him when he's the *only* thing I want. I thought I was doing the right thing...but now?

"I can't go back," I say, avoiding the question.

She rolls her eyes. "Sure you can. Just head on over then and ring his doorbell."

If only she knew how impossible that was. I mean, sure, he has a buzzer system. But that goes through the concierge. I couldn't surprise him unless I'd kept at least one of those magic beans. Probably two to operate the elevator. I never managed to do that myself.

No, I left them with him, along with Micky's contact details so he could improve his security system. If I were him, that's the first thing I'd do.

To keep little fuckers like me from breaking in.

"Oh, Mum," I say thickly, something inside me breaking. "I don't even have his number. Have I made a terrible mistake?"

She gets up and throws her arms around me like I'm an angry, grieving teenager once again. "Hey now, love. It's not too late to set things right, I promise. The way you lit up when you got talking about him...I've never seen you like that before. Do you think he has feelings for you, too? Or was it really just a fling?"

I chew on my lip, losing the battle with my tears. "He *begged* me to stay. He wanted to try and make it work. He wanted to take care of me."

She sighs even heavier than before. "So of course you ran a mile. Oh, my poor baby. It'll be all right. But you do need to fix it, okay?"

"Okay," I agree.

A voice in my head tries to pipe up that just because I have feelings for this man, it won't expunge my criminal record. Some things can't be repaired.

But I'm good at fixing things now. I'm not sure how, but she's right. I can fix this. I can at least tell him I love him, even if my past means we can't be together. There's a chance that he won't hate me.

So long as I haven't already broken everything beyond repair.

CHAPTER 21

Felix

I THINK I'D BUILT IT UP A LOT IN MY MIND THAT I WAS AFRAID of crowds. Intimidated by them, in fact. Somehow, I forgot that I'm at least a foot taller than almost everyone I pass by.

I'm the scary thing, not the other way around.

So I do my best to navigate the building lobby and the bustling London streets with a smile and a nod to anyone who looks my way. I know that's not really the done thing in this city. Londoners go about their business and absolutely do not make unsolicited chit-chat. But a higher-than-average percentage of people look my way—often as a double take—so I'm determined to be pleasant and as non-threatening as possible.

I haven't left The Beanstalk in months, and it never even bothered me. I have a gym in the building, can get anything I want delivered, and anyone I needed to talk to was always just a phone or Zoom call away.

Until Jack Spriggs walked out of my life a couple of hours ago, and I realised I had to conquer my fears or they were going to eat me alive.

At first, I was so angry at him I'd just stalked around the

place seething obscenities with Goose flying in circles around my head. I didn't know where I was going until I found myself standing in front of the restored coin collection, running my hands along the sides. I was still waiting for the custom cut glass top to finish it off, but Jack had done a wonderful job of putting everything back in its place.

And then some.

I'd blinked and raised my eyebrows when I realised there was an additional coin without a slot. It was just resting freely on the red velvet, and I'd picked it up to examine it. Why would he have left a simple British penny behind? It was completely unremarkable.

Until I'd looked at the date.

1993.

Understanding had hit me like a tidal wave. Realising it was from his birth year, I also recalled that he'd had a penny in his pocket when I'd made him turn them out after I first caught him in here. In that moment I just knew it was significant to him.

And he'd left it behind.

I'd really cursed his name then, squeezing the penny in my fist as my throat clamped and tears filled my eyes. Then my damn bird had started asking for Jack, saying "good boy, pretty boy, Jack, Jack!" and I'd stumbled upstairs, crumpled into the bed, and had a good sob.

When I surfaced, I noticed he'd left all the clothes I'd bought him, which hurt me unbelievably. But then it was as if all that crying had left me with a moment of clarity.

He didn't think he was good enough for me or my gifts.

How many times did he mention my money, my job, my penthouse in the clouds? All whilst calling himself a thief, nobody, nothing. He wouldn't believe it could be real because to him, it was so impossible.

But he was the best and most real thing that's happened to me in a long time.

I saw his face. Those tears. I think I let myself believe him when he said he wanted to walk away because I've been so terrified of relationships all this time, it seemed easier to let him go than to fight as much as I really wanted, only to get my heart ripped into shreds again.

Well, it's already been pretty badly torn. I can't imagine it'll get much worse, so once I got over my tantrum, I decided I needed to fight properly.

Because I would have fought to the ends of the Earth to have just one more day with Henry again, fit and healthy like when we first met. But I couldn't. No amount of money in the world could have done that, and I lost him. I watched him slip away before my very eyes.

I'm not losing the man I love again. Not this time.

I don't care that it's fast. I don't care that we're both terrified of being hurt by each other. Because what we're doing right now isn't working either. No, I'm in charge. It's my job to take care of him, so that's what I'm going to do.

I could have ordered a car to drive me anywhere I wanted, but a crazy whim came over me to navigate the underground. I haven't been on the tube literally for years, and I definitely got turned around several times. But I found myself having fun. I was on an adventure.

And now here I am, marching down a slightly less busy street, looking at the directions currently guiding me on my phone. Ah. This should be the place.

I make my way up to the front door and knock sharply. I take a breath and smooth down my shirt and coat, glad I forced myself to shower before setting off on this little escapade. After all that time hidden away, I wanted to look my best.

There's a shuffling sound behind the door as various

chains are moved around and locks turned. Then the door creaks open, and a lanky man with reddish-brown hair peeks out, a cigarette hanging from his lips.

His eyes widen when he takes me in. All of me.

"Oh, fuck right off!" he cries in a thick Aberdeen accent and tries to slam the door on me. Obviously, that doesn't go well for him. I thrust my hand out, stopping the door in its tracks. Then I jam my foot between the door and its frame.

"Micky Muir, I presume?" I say cheerfully.

"Um, no," he says, his eyes flicking back and forth as he drags on the fag, making the end flare bright red. "Don't know who tha' is, but um…"

I chuckle. "You're not in trouble, Mr Muir. In fact, I have a proposition for you. May I come in?" I indicate the balcony of the council estate I'm currently standing on. "Not really the ideal location to conduct business."

"Um…"

"Jolly good," I say, flashing a smile and forcing my way over the threshold. I find myself directly in a living room filled with enough humming computer equipment to power the BBC's entire TV network. I ignore that and stride into the kitchen. There are an unusual amount of frog-themed items scattered about. I do my best not to quirk an amused smile. "Tea?"

"Nah, I'm good," he says with a dismissive wave.

My grin broadens. "I would like some tea."

Micky blinks for a second, then launches himself at the kettle, flicking it on and grabbing a mug covered in footballs from a nearby cupboard. "Milk, sugar?" he says quickly as he stubs his fag out in the sink. He's not a bad-looking fellow. He's actually quite ruggedly handsome. But I only have room in my heart for one little submissive thief, so I enjoy Micky's obedience in an abstract way.

"Yes, both," I say, leaning against a counter.

There's an awkward silence as he determinedly watches the water boil. I wait until he's finished making my brew and hands it to me. I take a sip, sigh, then finally feel ready to talk.

"I've had a pretty bad day," I start off.

"Whadya do wi' Jack?" Micky blurts out. I realise he's armed himself with a butter knife. "Didya hurt him? I swear—"

I use the hand not holding the tea to wave him quiet. "Jack is absolutely fine—last I saw him, anyway." I won't go into the heartbreak. That's not really the point of this conversation.

"You are Felix Fagiolo, though, yeah?" he asks with an arched eyebrow.

"The one and only," I confirm.

"Jack sent a message days ago…?"

I nod and sip my tea again. He put two sugars in without checking with me, so it's a little sweet. But after the exhausting morning I've had, I actually kind of appreciate the kick it gives me.

"Yes, when I caught him red-handed in my safe, trying to rip me off. Know anything about that?"

"Umm…" His eyes flick to the front door, and I tsk to myself. I need to stop teasing the poor man.

"It's fine," I assure him. "He agreed to fix the damage he'd caused, and I didn't call the authorities. We became… friends." That was such an inadequate word, but I really don't feel like going into the details now.

Micky licks his lips and finally lowers his knife. "Okay?" he says uncertainly.

"Jack didn't give you up," I explain. "However, he did strongly imply that if I wanted someone to take a look at my security system and make it bulletproof, you might just be the man for the job…seeing as you were the one who got him inside in the first place."

He drops the knife into the sink and pulls on a loose thread on his woolly jumper. "Who says I did anything of the sort?"

"Me," I say, flashing my smile at him again before sipping more of my sugary tea. "The point is moot, though. Judging by the fact that you have the inside of the T.A.R.D.I.S. currently operating in your living room, I'd say you know a fair thing or two about computers. Can you help me or not?"

Micky puffs out his chest and folds his arms. "Och, ai. I could mebe help you out. It'll cost you, though."

"How does a hundred thousand pounds sound?"

For a good few moments, Micky Muir doesn't move a muscle. "Uhhh…?"

"All above board and on the books, of course," I say. "So you'd have to pay tax on it."

He hums again, and I have a feeling he will most certainly *not* pay the tax on my payment, but that really isn't any of my concern.

"An' you won't tell the coppers?" he asks, narrowing his eyes.

I raise my eyebrows. "About what, Mr Muir?"

He smirks, nods, and licks his lips as he taps his chin. I can practically see his mind whirling. "Howdya know I won't screw you over?"

I have considered this, and I already know my answer.

"Jack trusts you, so I trust you," I say. And I mean it. If this little shit has any common sense or hint of self-preservation, he'll recognise a good thing when he sees one.

Micky regards me for another few seconds. "Because you two are such good…*pals* now?"

"Exactly," I say with a neutral smile. "Besides, if you screw me over, this time I'll *definitely* cart you off to jail. Understood?"

He glares at me, but there's also a sparkle in his shifty eyes. "An' Jack?"

"What about him?"

"He doesn't go back ta prison, either. He's not built for it."

I get the feeling I suddenly know where Jack and Micky met. I like that even though this man is evidently the poster child for 'morally grey', he cares about Jack. That's the second time he's defended and protected him since I arrived.

Anyone willing to protect Jack is all right in my book.

"Jack is one hundred percent not going back to prison," I agree, my heart aching at the mere thought of it. "But whilst we're on the subject, I believe there is something else you could help me with regarding our mutual friend."

"Jack?" he says, and I nod. "You pay him off, too?"

At that, my smile falters, and I shake my head. "He wouldn't take a penny." Literally. He left his behind.

Micky smirks. "Stupid, stubborn bastard." He sounds extremely proud.

"Jack and I have our own business," I say, grinning again. "Let's close the matter between you and me. You do me a favour as well as updating my security system, then we'll forget all about the minor issue of aiding and abetting a rather significant crime."

He looks me up and down. "An' my money?"

"I'll pay you as soon as my home is safe once more."

He considers me a little longer, then nods. "Go on, then. What's this other favour?"

I name my price.

CHAPTER 22
Jack

THE LAST THING I FEEL LIKE DOING IS GOING AND MEETING Micky. But he's insisting that I come to some bar that he's sent me the address to so that we can discuss things, and he won't take no for an answer. I eventually decide that it would be best to get the conversation over and done with. He's not going to be happy anyway, so I might as well be honest upfront.

It's not like he could possibly be any unhappier than I am.

Mum kindly let me crash on her sofa and made me some soup when I woke up, so I don't feel terrible as I venture once more out into the evening. I really don't want to go back into central, but I tell myself that if I take this quick-ish detour, I'll be home soon enough.

The thought doesn't bring me all that much comfort. There's nothing really for me where I've been living, although I guess I can stop worrying about my meds supply. It gives me anxiety, knowing I don't have any spares, but I can always skip one and in theory it'll be fine.

I'd rather not test that out, though.

One quick drink, I tell myself, and then I can try and put

this whole big mess behind me. I honestly can't believe that this time last week, I was psyching myself up to pull off one of the biggest jobs I've ever attempted, and this time yesterday, I was preparing myself to make love with Felix for the last time.

Wow. My life might suck, but at least it's not boring, I guess.

I jump on the District Line with all the people already heading out of work. I pass the time staring out of the window at the black tunnel walls between the stops that rush past. Eventually, I hop off to exit near St James's Park, wondering why Micky's chosen this particular neck of the woods rather than one of our usual haunts. Dodgy pubs seem appropriate places to do dodgy dealings.

When I reach the entrance, I look between the sign above the door and the address on my phone that gave me the map directions. This can't be right? Can it? It looks more like a fancy wine bar than a pub. Is Micky planning on *robbing* it?

I'm so unsure that I retreat a few paces back and fire off a message at Micky, hoping he's got an eye on his phone.

JACK: Is this the right place?

Three dots appear almost immediately.

MICKY: Just get inside, dickhead.

I roll my eyes and take a deep breath, putting my mobile back in my pocket and gripping the handles of my rucksack for a bit of support. "Let's get it over with," I mumble to myself.

As I head inside, I try not to get overwhelmed with how much I feel like I don't belong. At least I'm still in all black, so that doesn't look too scruffy. But from the overhead chandelier to the woman in a sharp black suit behind the host's podium, I definitely feel like everyone here is going to judge the shit out of me.

Well, if they're judging me, they're definitely judging Micky. So I steel myself and walk onwards.

The lady behind the desk doesn't even flinch as she looks up and gives me a big smile. "Good evening, sir. How can I help you?"

The 'sir' almost makes me laugh. It would have if I wasn't so miserable. But I muster a small smile, very grateful she didn't take one look at the commoner and kick him out.

"I'm meeting a friend," I say.

She nods and looks down at what I assume to be a list. "Can I please take your name?"

My name? I'd have thought she'd want Micky's name. But how the hell would I know how places like this work? "Jack Spriggs."

She looks for a second, then nods, her smile still genuine. "Wonderful. If you'll follow me, I can show you to your table."

I try not to gulp as we walk through an archway into the bar proper. It's filled with small tables and velvet-lined booths, and the lighting is low, giving it a very cosy air. A man in a tuxedo is playing a gentle melody on a black grand piano to my left. He doesn't have a top hat on, but still. My jaw hangs open slightly as I stare, almost walking into a table because I'm so mesmerised by him.

From their seats, a couple of women in cocktail dresses— *cocktail dresses*—snap their heads around as I throw my hands up. "I'm so sorry," I hiss.

But one of the ladies just beams at me. "He's very good, isn't he," she says enthusiastically, jutting her chin towards the pianist.

"Enjoy your night," says the other one kindly.

"Um, thanks."

I blink, then continue to follow the host as she weaves

through more tables. That was strange. Why were they nice to me?

The host suddenly spins around to face me. "Here you go, Mr Spriggs," she says, indicating a corner table. "Your waiter will be with you shortly. Please let them know if you need anything at all."

She nods and sweeps past me, which is a good thing because I'm frozen to the spot.

It's not Micky waiting for me at the table.

It's Felix.

He's staring right back at me, and I see him inhale deeply and slowly. Then he turns his hand over so his palm is facing the ceiling, indicating the empty seat opposite him. There's a bottle of Champagne in a silver bucket in the centre of the table as well as two full glasses waiting in front of each of the chairs.

My head is swimming. What the fuck is happening? How can Felix be here—outside? Where's Micky?

"He's not coming," Felix says as if reading my mind. "He and I struck a deal."

"You w-what?" I splutter as I creep closer.

The corner of Felix's mouth twitches, but then his expression smooths out again. "He's going to make my security system burglary-proof, remember? In turn, I asked him to send a few text messages for me."

Oh, fuck. It's all a set-up. "I'm going to kill Micky," I say weakly as I slink into the empty chair.

That does get a light chuckle from Felix. "Hello again, Jack," he says softly.

I close my eyes. "Did you change your mind?" I ask, my voice a mere croak. "Have you called the police?"

"Called the—*Jack!*" He sounds irritated and exasperated, and I can't help but peek through my eyelids again. Then he laughs properly and runs a hand through his hair. "I'm furious at you, yes. But no, I still haven't called the authorities, and I never will."

"Okay," I say, looking around and feeling completely confused. "You, um, left the penthouse."

He looks at his finger and thumb as he runs them up and down the stem of his Champagne flute. I resist the urge to shiver, even though the sight is totally hot. "Yes, I did," he answers my question. "For you."

My mouth goes dry. "For…me?" I squeak.

"Apparently, I didn't make myself clear this morning, Jack," he says quietly, his eyes still on his drink. "But I love you. And I don't believe you when you say you don't want to be with me. I think you're afraid you're not my equal because of your financial status, but that isn't true. You're not my equal because I'm your Dom, and I *worship the ground you walk on.*"

His eyes flash at me, blazing in a way I've never seen before. It takes my breath away, and I tremble, barely able to nod my head. Rational thought has left the building and all I can think is that I don't want to disappoint him.

"Y-yes, Sir. I'm sorry, Sir," I manage to utter.

His expression immediately melts. "Good boy," he murmurs.

"My mum thinks I'm an idiot," I blurt out.

"I knew I liked your mum," he says softly, his gaze still trained on me. "Would you like to explain your behaviour? You made me cry, you know."

I let out a whine, my skin feeling hot and tingly. I grip the edge of my seat and try and scramble my thoughts into any kind of cohesive order.

In the end, I just know that my mum was right.

"Nothing hurt me like the pain for my dad dying," I say in a rush so I don't chicken out. "I couldn't face the thought of someone I loved leaving me again, so I always ran away from nice guys and fucked the bastards instead." I grit my teeth and fight back the tears. "You were the nicest guy, so I left you the hardest. I ran away. I couldn't stand the thought that you'd hurt me, but instead, I hurt you when you've already had your heart ripped out, and for that, I can never, ever be sorry enough."

For a moment, he just looks at me. Then he takes a breath and puts his large hand out on the table between us. I practically throw my little one into it, and he wraps his fingers around mine, squeezing tightly.

"I'm scared, too, baby," he tells me. "So scared. The only other man I ever loved was taken from me. So I had to fight for you, even if it meant playing dirty. I'm never going to make you stay anywhere you don't want to be. But tell me the truth right now. No games. Do you want to be with me?"

I'm not strong enough. I can't lie a second time. Not when Mum knocked some sense into me and he's here, now, making a grand gesture to try and win me back. But I have to check something first.

"What about my criminal record?" I ask. "I've done time in prison. People will find out. I can't stand the thought of that hurting you or your reputation, Felix."

He raises his eyebrows. "What's anyone going to do?" he asks, a sparkle in his beautiful blue eyes. "Lock me up in a tower and never speak to me again?" I can't help the mildly hysterical laugh that escapes my throat, and he nods at me. "Exactly. I have the luxury of being rich enough not to give a shit. My wealth doesn't depend on other people's good opinion of me. If they have a problem with that, I don't want to associate with them anyway. So I'll ask you again. Ignoring all of that, do you want to be with me? Because if you weren't a thief we never would have met, Jack Spriggs, so I can wholeheartedly tell you I don't give a flying fuck about your past. Only your future—with me."

The damn breaks. "I want to be with you more than anything," I whimper.

He makes a strange sound, his face crumpling before he yanks me to my feet and into his arms so he can hug the shit out of me.

"You still smell like the aftershave I bought you," he mumbles into my chest.

I let out a broken laugh. "I drenched myself in it this morning," I admit sheepishly. "I wanted to take the bottle but felt like I couldn't. So instead, I used as much as I could without choking on it, hoping it would last a few days so I'd have something to remember you by."

Felix lets out an aching sigh and presses our foreheads together. "Oh, Jack. My poor little one."

"I'm so sorry, Felix," I sob as I cling to him. I don't care who's looking at us. We're in a dark corner. Anyone watching should mind their own business.

His fingers dig into my back. "No, *I'm* sorry, Jack. I should have taken better care of you. Supported you more."

I draw back to look at him, horrified. "More? Felix, you did everything for me."

For the one and only time since I've met him, he looks old as he regards me with glassy eyes. "It wasn't enough to make you want to stay, though."

I throw myself back around him, cursing how useless I am. "I wanted to. I promise. I just thought I couldn't."

"One of the perks of being a literal billionaire is that I make my own bloody rules," Felix grumbles, and I can't help but laugh despite my tears.

"It doesn't sound right when you're grumpy," I protest.

He threads his fingers through my hair and holds me tight. "Say you'll come home, and I'll never be grumpy again."

I want to fight it. I'm still scared. Logically, I don't think I can possibly accept moving into his fancy-as-fuck penthouse after only knowing each other for a week.

But my heart is too tired to care about logic anymore. Life is too short, too precious. None of us know how long we really have left. Why am I running away from the best thing that's ever happened to me?

"I'll come home," I say thickly against his neck.

His embrace is crushing, but I kind of like the pain.

Apparently, that's my thing.

"I'll take care of your mum," he says firmly before I can even form the thought. "No arguing. You love her, so I love her. That's it. And before you even say the bloody words, I've already had six months of your medication delivered to my home. We can pack up your things from your current place and have them delivered as well, but I want to buy you more clothes. A whole wardrobe. I don't plan on you ever wanting for anything again."

I shake my head, hung up on it despite what he said. "My meds? But you don't have my prescription."

He leans back and gives me a withering look. "What's the point of being filthy rich if I can't bend the rules every now and again?"

My eyes go wide. "You...are they...did you...?"

"Get them off the back of a truck? Yes." He flashes a grin at me. "Anything for you, baby."

I smack his arm. "You're supposed to be the good one!"

He shrugs and suddenly pulls me into his lap. I know we're in a shadowy corner, but I still gasp and look around the room, scandalised. "What if someone sees?"

He hums and kisses my neck. *Fuck.* I thought I'd never have this again, and have to fight back a wave of emotion.

"If anyone complains, I'll just buy the bloody bar," he gripes.

I can't tell if he's joking or not.

"I'm sorry, Felix," I say quietly again after a time.

"I know, sweetheart. Please listen when I say it's okay. We're both broken. We're both hurting. But I think together, we can heal."

I nod and inhale his scent deep into my lungs. How could I ever think it would be possible to forget him?

He strokes my back. "Jack?"

I hum.

"I've got a present for you. Is that okay?"

I sigh and nod again with a little chuckle. "I promise I will work very hard on letting you spoil me from now on. It's difficult for me, largely because I'm afraid of how much I love it."

Felix fucking beams at me. "Excellent. I'm going to remind you that you said that frequently, okay?"

I laugh but shrug, knowing this is a losing battle.

He encourages me to sit back in my seat, which I think is probably good, as my poor body is so confused. I'm a shaky mess, but my cock is also doing its very best to get excited. So I'm relieved to have just the smallest bit of space for now.

He reaches in between his chair and the wall, pulling out a black box. It's only a couple of inches deep but a couple of feet wide and long, making a reasonably large but shallow rectangle. It has a silver bow on it, and I accept it with trembling hands, moving my untouched drink and placing it down on the table.

"What's this?" I ask.

He shakes his head, but his expression is extremely fond. "You have to open it to find out. That's how presents work."

"Smart-arse," I grumble, but I'm still grinning as I carefully pull the top off the cardboard box.

And then all the air evaporates from my lungs as my eyes fill with tears.

Inside, neatly folded up on silver tissue paper, is my dad's jacket.

"How did you…?"

Felix reaches over and gently slides his hand over mine. "Micky was happy to give it to me once he understood the circumstances."

I arch an eyebrow. "Did you pay him money?"

"An *obscene* amount of money," Felix says without skipping a beat, a big grin still splattered over his face.

I laugh, but it turns into a sob. "Thank you," I say, my voice cracking as I hug the leather to my chest. "This means more to me than you could possibly know."

Felix sighs and shakes his head. "Baby, of course I know how much it means to you. That's the whole fucking point."

I let out a too-loud laugh as tears spill down my face. "Take me home, Felix. Please. Take me home and make me yours."

He lifts my hand with his own and kisses my fingers. "You're already mine, sweetheart. But nothing would give me more pleasure than to take you *home*."

Home.

Where I belong.

CHAPTER 23

Jack

PEOPLE STARE AT US AS WE WALK HAND IN HAND.

I don't care.

In fact, I kind of love how unusual we look as a couple because everything about us is unusual. Unique. I wouldn't have it any other way.

I think we each needed something extraordinary to come along and shake us out of our ways. We were both stuck. But now we've set each other free.

It's a completely different elevator ride up to the penthouse than I took last time. Felix uses his own fob to operate it, then grins at me, ignoring the other people standing with us. "Won't be able to use this for much longer," he says with a wink, and my stomach flips over at his silly flirting.

I texted my mum as we left the wine bar to let her know I'd un-fucked the situation, and she was so ridiculously happy for me. She wants to meet Felix as soon as possible, of course. But her happiness also reinforced my happiness. It reminded me of just how lucky I am to have been given this second chance.

I don't intend on wasting it this time.

I'm glad Felix didn't take his wrath out on Micky. The man deserved a payday for the magic he worked on the fobs he sourced for me. And I really don't have the words to express my gratitude that he gave Felix back my dad's leather jacket. I knew he wasn't a malicious person, but him holding it hostage had left me feeling very distressed.

I pull the collar up to my face and inhale the warm smell of it. My other coat is in the silver box, but I still have enough of Felix's aftershave on my T-shirt that the two scents—old and new—mingle together to create something new.

It strikes me that the aftershave isn't Felix's. It's mine now, for real. And the jacket hasn't belonged to my dad for a long time. That's also mine. They belong to the new person I'm becoming because I've met the most incredible man who believes in me.

I can't wait to get to know myself better than I ever have in my whole life.

Like before, we're the only ones left in the lift by the time it dings, indicating that we've reached the top level. I glance up at Felix and find him looking down at me.

"We're home, little one," he says softly.

Excitement and anticipation bubble inside me as we cross the lobby to get to his—*our*—front door. I'm tired from such a long, emotional day, but I'm also vibrating as we head inside, definitely not ready to sleep anytime soon.

It appears that Felix has the same idea. After he closes the door, he wordlessly pulls me up the stairs. I expect him to take me to the bedroom. I get chills thinking about how all my stuff is still there, waiting for me. I didn't think I'd see any of it again, but now it's all really mine.

Just like Felix is.

Instead, he keeps pulling me along the hallway, and I realise we're heading back out onto the terrace. I haven't been back out here since our date. It's been cleared of all the dinner things, but the fairy lights are still set up and lit, and the heaters come on, triggered by our movements, I guess.

Felix whirls on me, picking me up easily as I yelp. But I get over the surprise pretty quickly, wrapping my legs around his thick waist and my arms around his neck as our mouths come crashing together in a frantic kiss.

"I thought I'd lost you," he mumbles against my lips.

"I'm sorry, so sorry," I gasp.

He hums, low and dangerous in a way that goes straight to my balls. "You've been a bad, *bad* boy, Jack."

"I'm sorry, Sir. I'll be good for you now. I *promise.*"

"Yes, you will," he agrees, a savage grin on his face before he bites my lower lip and drags it through his teeth. "My good boy."

He sits me on the table, and I realise that the bottle of lube is resting on one of the chairs. "You were pretty confident I was going to say yes and come back," I note with a relieved giggle.

He grunts as he shucks my jacket off my shoulders. "We both fucked up. I was going to drag you back here like a caveman if I had to so I could prove that to you."

"Why is that so hot?" I moan, still grinning as he pulls my jumper and T-shirt off together. I'm naked from the waist up now as he leans down and kisses me again.

"You're hot," he growls. "Mine. *My* little thief." There's that monosyllabic neanderthal again. God, I thought I'd lost him.

I sigh as he kisses my neck, his large hands stroking my sides. "All yours," I agree.

Abruptly, he pushes me to lie on my back before attacking my trouser fly. Oh, wow. He's really getting me naked up here out in the open, isn't he? We're so high up, and night has fallen, but still, I feel so exposed as he strips me down to my bare skin.

He crowds on top of me, hovering over my body and capturing my mouth with a filthy kiss. The table is cold on my skin, not to mention the October breeze that slips through the glass panels shielding the balcony. The heaters are good. However, they can only do so much against the elements.

But I like it. The stark contrast between the coldness around me and the heat of his body is electrifying. Besides, I'm his to do with as he pleases. He owns me. I don't have any choice but to surrender and accept whatever he wants to do to me.

I feel so free.

He surprises me as he hauls me to sit back up again. Then he picks up my leather jacket and helps me slip it back on. "Perfect," he says. I'm too choked with emotion to say anything, so I just nod. He sees me for who I really am. All my flaws and pain. And he still wants me.

He still loves me.

I still can't believe he said that back at the bar, but in my heart, I can't deny it to be true. Largely because as crazy as it might sound, I already know I love him right back. I'm his grumpy little thief, and he's my cheerful giant. The most unlikely, perfect couple.

He takes my hand and gently tugs it so I slide off the table and walk barefoot with him over to the edge of the terrace, looking out over what feels like the whole of London glittering in the darkness, putting on a spectacle that only we can see.

He shoves me against the glass, my cheek and torso pressed against it, as he leans his front against my back and nips at my earlobe.

"You're going to stay right there whilst I fuck you for the whole world to see," he growls. I shiver all over and moan. "You're *mine*, Jacks Spriggs. Let the gods above and the mortals below watch on as I fucking claim you. I'm going to destroy you so you'll never, ever think about running away again."

I let out a whine and nod as best I can. "Y-yes, Sir. Please. Oh, *fuck.*"

Suddenly, his body is no longer crowding mine as he drops to his knees. I want to tell him to grab a pillow to protect his joints, but he's already pulling my arse cheeks apart, and I lose all coherent thought as he wastes no time in feasting on my hole.

I squeal and yelp, still pretty sore and stretched out from making love last night. But that only means it doesn't take him long to get me just how he wants me.

He spanks my arse cheek hard, making me bellow. I'm still tender from the first spanking. "Don't move," he warns.

I laugh weakly. I'm not going anywhere. There's no place on Earth I'd rather be, even if my jelly legs were capable of movement.

He's soon back, lube-drenched fingers shoving inside me, coating my insides and my crack so I'm as slippery as possible to accept his enormous cock. He withdraws his hand and wipes his fingers on his trousers. I glance back and watch as he unzips his fly and shoves his clothes down just enough to free his dick. He takes one hand and angles it up with my entrance, then splays the other over my stomach, digging his fingers into my flesh as he starts to breach me.

"You're mine, Jack," he snarls as I pant and shudder.

My hands slap against the glass, and I look down at the streets below. Vertigo swoops through me, and instinctively I try and flinch away. But Felix's huge, solid body has got me trapped. There's nothing between me and a five-hundred-foot fall but one sheet of safety glass and the strong grip he has on me.

I know I'm safe. But my heart is slamming in my chest, and I'm gasping for air all the same.

"I love you, Jack," he says as he penetrates deeper. He's also biting and sucking on my neck, marking me. "You're all mine. I'll take care of you, baby. Always. The whole world is going to know you belong to me, and you'll never want for anything again. Fuck, *fuck.*"

"Holy shit, Felix, yes! Yes, *Sir.*"

He's already thrusting into me, filling me up, setting off fireworks every time he strokes my prostate. His other hand is now digging into my hip as he uses my body to pleasure himself thoroughly. He moves from holding my belly to gripping my cock. It jerks in his hand, and I flail and cry out as he starts to vigorously wank me off.

"Come for me, baby," he rasps in my ear. "Come for all of London. Show them who you are, who you belong to."

I scream under his relentless assault, giving in as my climax comes crashing over me. Cum splatters against the glass, and Felix roars as he fills up my arse with his seed. I'm his, all his, completely and utterly.

He holds me tight for a while, his strong arms keeping me on my feet when I want to melt into a puddle. Soon, he'll pick me up and take me down to the main bathroom, where we'll soak in a scorching hot tub, the sweet-scented water covered in red rose petals. Then we'll spend the night in our enormous bed, where he'll make love to me whenever and however he wants.

But for just a few minutes longer, we stay on the terrace with him buried deep inside me, the stars above us and the city below, floating in the clouds in our own private heaven.

"My little thief," he murmurs into my ear. "You stole my heart."

I shake my head. "You gave your heart to me willingly,

Felix, and I promise to always take care of it. Just like you'll always take care of mine."

He nods, and I turn my head enough for him to give me a gentle kiss. "I promise," he says.

This is our vow that we make in front of all the world to see. I've broken many things in my life, but I know I'll *never* break that.

Epilogue

FELIX – TWO YEARS LATER

I STEP OUT INTO THE SUNSHINE, CLOSING MY EYES AS I FEEL the breeze touch my face, hearing as it rustles the leaves in the trees around me.

Glorious.

Jack and I split our time these days between the penthouse in London and our new cottage here in the Lake District. I say 'cottage'. It is still two storeys and three thousand square feet, and that's not including the fields, woodlands, and the stream that are technically public land that give us peaceful surroundings in all directions.

I glance back to make sure the door is closed properly behind me so that Goose is safe. He loves that we have a second home now, and every time we come up here, he spends his time singing as he explores all the nooks and crannies, all while calling Jack a 'good boy' because even my bird knows that Jack is the one responsible for all of this.

My little one. My darling. He looks up from the patio table that stands a few dozen feet away from me down the short path, near the hot tub that we've put to good use on countless occasions. He's got the table all set up with food and decorations, and when he sees me, he waves enthusiastically with both arms.

"Happy fiftieth birthday!" he yells, running down the path to greet me by throwing his arms around me. I have two cups of tea in my hands. Otherwise, I'd pick him up and spin him around. Instead, I settle for kissing him deeply.

He's still my grumpy thief at heart, but I can't deny that I love seeing how much he smiles these days.

I love every single thing about my tiny husband.

His wedding band catches the morning light as he steps back and takes one of the mugs from me, smiling as he has a quick sip.

Copper plated steel is an unusual choice for rings, I'll admit. But it was easy enough for me to source a penny minted in my birth year of 1975 to match his lucky 1993 coin, and then I had them melted down and made more durable by forming a ring over a core of steel. Now, he wears my penny every day, and I his.

They're already starting to turn green, but in my opinion that just gives them a beautiful antique look. Besides, I *want* to be reminded that time is passing. That we're here, living our lives, together.

Last summer, we realised that both of us had lost too much already in this world and didn't want to waste any more time than we had already. We had a small, debaucherous ceremony and party at The Ritz with his mum and a few of our friends. Micky was Jack's best man. He seemed baffled by the whole thing and definitely nicked god knows how much stuff from the place. But I believe that added to the thoroughly good time that was had by all.

Then I whisked Jack off to Bali for a month, where we spent the whole time fucking like rabbits, eating and drinking to our hearts' content, and simply watching the sun set over the waves. After we came home, we started to look for the perfect country residence to buy for whenever we wanted to escape the hustle and bustle of the city.

Now I've taken a back seat with the company, it's not like I need to be in London all the time anyway. I didn't really before as it was, operating mostly via Zoom. That's not changed. But I have.

Without the day-to-day minutia of being a CEO dragging me down for the first time in years, I'm rediscovering what makes me happy. Jack encouraged me to take an Open University history degree that I can study for at my own leisure, and I'm planning on one day writing a book about the evolution of commerce and physical currency. I doubt anyone would ever read such a thing, but it will delight me no end. One day, I'll be able to hold 'my little book of coins' in my own hands, the perfect accompaniment to my ever growing historical collection.

Of course, I made sure before I stepped back that the Dagenham branch was fully up and running again, operating better than ever. We retained about eighty percent of the original staff, including Jack's mum, who I unashamedly promoted to a managerial position. The woman is more than qualified regardless, but when I made it so she could use voice-to-text technology for most of her work, there was no stopping her. With Jack's permission, I also bought her a brand new flat that she owns outright close to the plant. She'll never have to worry about damp or greedy landlords ever again.

I inhale the clear morning air and look around the garden. I'm only just getting started in cultivating it how I want it, but the simple novelty of having my own dirt to dig my fingers into is mind blowing. This isn't like my other family properties. It's all mine. Just like Jack.

We've been talking about maybe selling some of those other houses. I never use them anyway. The ancestral manor

I want to turn over to National Heritage. It's always felt like a museum to me, so why not open it to the public?

No. The penthouse and the cottage are all we need. I love it here, but I'm sure I'd love anywhere Jack is. Still, it always makes me ridiculously happy every time we visit, and there was nowhere else I wanted to be for my big five-oh.

Jack excitedly takes my hand and drags me towards the breakfast spread he secretly set up before I woke up. I suspect he tired me out last night specifically so I'd sleep in. I can't say I'm mad about his plan.

"I know you said you didn't want any presents or fuss or anything," he starts off by saying.

I roll my eyes and hug him to me as we approach the table. "No, I don't need anything except you, baby. But this looks beautiful. Thank you."

He blushes as I kiss his cheek. Of all the things my husband has found a passion for now he's a man of leisure, one of his favourites is flower arranging. The display that's interspersed between all the plates of food make it look like some kind of Grecian fest worthy of Dionysus, the god of wine, orgies, and general good times.

I fucking adore that Jack's hobbies these days are based around things of pure beauty. He's been allowed to spread his wings now he's not consumed with the worry of paying his bills or looking after his mum all the time. He paints and takes dance classes and has even started his own collection of teapots. The ones I buy him are expensive and rare. But he's equally happy with chipped ones he finds in charity shops or quirky designs he buys online.

He just…shines now. It's the greatest gift I could ever ask for.

"Yes, well," he huffs. I love that his grumpiness is always lurking there under the surface if I poke hard enough. "I'm not *not* going to celebrate your birthday, baby. I've wrapped up a few silly things for you." He indicates a small pile. The boxes are black with silver bows, just like the wrapping I had for giving him back his dad's leather jacket. "And we're going out to that posh steakhouse tonight. But before that, I've decided you get to fuck me all day in the most lavish, obscene ways you can think of."

I drop my head back and laugh, my cock already warming to that idea. "Is that so?"

He grins and stands on his tiptoes, asking for a kiss, which I gladly give him. "Yup. The house is littered with fun stuff. There are outfits and everything."

I hum and kiss him again. "Now that's the kind of present I'm interested in."

He beams at me, but then his expression turns shy. "You'll have to be a *bit* gentle with me, though."

I raise my eyebrows. "Are you okay, sweetheart?"

Dammit—did I hurt him? There have been a few pulled muscles on occasions where my lust for him became a little unhinged. So long as he can recover quickly, both of us quite enjoy that. It's another way for me to mark and claim him. But I don't remember him making any complaints recently.

"I'm wonderful," he says, shaking his head to reassure me. "It's just…" He huffs then smiles brightly at me, making my heart melt for the millionth, billionth time. "Well, you were so adamant that you didn't want me to buy you things I hope you don't think this is a weird kind of present."

To my surprise, he steps back and starts pulling his T-shirt over his head. It's wonderfully warm for September, but still, it's hardly the beach.

Then I realise what he's showing me.

At the base of his throat where his collar bones meet are two new tattoos. I take a step closer, peering at the circular designs. They're highly detailed, so even though they're covered in protective clingfilm it only takes me a second to realise they're of our original 1993 and 1975 pennies. The skin is red around the ink, showing he must have just got them done. Perhaps a very early appointment in town before the shops even technically opened?

My eyes well up. "That's for me?" I whisper.

He nods before taking my hand and gently placing it over his newly branded flesh. "I'm yours, remember? So here's a little something to celebrate that."

I look at my large hand that's placed over his small one, our wedding bands standing out next to one another as they rest against his new tattoo. I don't regret melting down his lucky penny to make my ring one bit, and I know he doesn't, either. But now we can still see those two coins any time we want because he's captured them forever.

"I can't think of a more perfect gift," I say thickly.

A strange twist of fate might have brought us together, but we've fought so hard to stay by each other's sides, and I have no doubt we'll be as one for the rest of our lives. He saved me. I saved him. Together, we're flourishing and growing into something neither of us thought we could be.

The little thief and the giant billionaire. It sounds like some kind of crazy fairy tale. But this is real, the most real thing to happen to either of us, and we're going to keep our promise to each other every day to keep fixing our broken hearts.

I think of them like broken Japanese vases that have been put back together using gold, making them more beautiful than they were before. That's what we are. Two damaged souls made more perfect by their repair. We don't try and hide our cracks. We let the gold shine through.

I made a vow to spend the rest of my life caring for and protecting the man who crashed into my life and stole my heart. I look at his new, beautiful tattoos and thank every power in the universe that drew us together. He brought me back to life, so I'm going to spend the rest of our time together showing him it was worth it.

That he is worth it. If I lost it all, I'd give him my last penny. But really, wealth is neither here nor there. I'm rich because I have him. Together we can rule the clouds and grow our roots deep into the ground. This world is ours.

Forever.

————

Thank you so much for reading Jack and Felix's story! If you can, I hope you'll consider leaving a review. Word of mouth helps authors enormously. Turn the page for more fairy tale adaptations as well as books from my other pen name, HJ Welch!

————

Thank you to my team!
    Cover Design: Cate Ashwood
    Editing: Meg Cooper
    Proof Reading: Tanja Ongkiehong
    Formatting (and general awesomeness): Ed Davies
    Love and support: Hubby and our cats

he can't miss this opportunity, not even when his past comes back to haunt him.

————

Wild Ride

When Red is chased into the woods, he seeks sanctuary at his estranged grandma's house. He doesn't expect to be rescued by his older brother's best friend, the man he was always madly in love with. Could Hunter be the Daddy of Red's wildest dreams? Especially when he unlocks a secret passion of Red's for beautiful lingerie. There's still a threat lurking in the woods, though, and Hunter realises he'll do anything to protect his beautiful boy.

————

Three

When three shy best friends sign up to a dating app to finally get some by the end of the year, they don't expect to all fall for the same gorgeous, slightly scary-looking Daddy. The only solution? Let him choose who he wants to bed. Except he doesn't. Daddy Wolf wants to spoil each little piggy, one after another. But when danger comes calling, will their love for each other be enough to save them all?
Includes Halloween bonus scene!

————

Nine Lives

When Charlie suddenly finds himself homeless and penniless, he decides to sell the only thing left he owns. Himself. For the very first time. Lucky for him he stumbles across Miller, the own of a London kink club, who saves him from those who would take advantage of him. As Miller discovers his inner Daddy, he also unlocks Charlie's kitten alter-ego. But with both their families meddling, will new love be enough to keep them together?

Click here to get the Daddy's Fairy Tales Box Set

Thorn in His Side

Beautiful, innocent Joshua Bellamy finds himself in an arranged marriage to the older, brutish, and scarred Darius Legrand. But in Darius's secluded mansion, Joshua begins to see that Darius isn't so scary after all. In fact, despite being a little grumpy, he's actually very protective and caring. When danger comes knocking on their door, will Joshua and Darius's blossoming love be strong enough to save each other?

A Right Royal Affair

Nobody knows that Prince James of the United Kingdom is bisexual, and as he's sixth in line to the throne, it needs to stay that way. But when he meets the cheeky, outrageously gay Essex boy, Theo Glass, everything could change. Against his better judgement, James asks Theo to help him put on a royal charity ball to remember. Can they resist their mutual attraction for a whole week alone in a picturesque castle, or will true love bloom?

Hair Out of Place

Raphael d'Oro is a secret prince who has spent his entire life exiled in a London penthouse. But now he's in a race against time to get back to his tiny European nation to claim the throne that's rightfully his and save his people. Good thing he has his insanely hot older bodyguard to take care of him. But Griff Thompson would never want someone as inexperienced as Raphie, would he? Even *if* they keep finding themselves in places with only one bed…

Click here for the Fairy Tale Collection eBook

Click here for the Fairy Tale Collection audio

PADDLE CREEK #1: HEAVEN SENT BY HJ WELCH

Two rival jocks. One adorable nerd. A bet that changes everything.

SETH

Being captain of the Paddle Creek Panthers is my life. I wouldn't care that my grades have slipped, except it could not only cost me my shot at the pros, but now the rich kid in town has wagered that if I don't graduate, I'll owe him *big* time. Can this gorgeous little freshman geek Gabe really save my degree and my reputation? All I know is that as soon as I laid eyes on him, I needed him. And I *don't* want to share.

MARTY

I've spent almost four years trying to get my captain Seth to notice me. He's hot as hell and knows how to boss a guy around, even one as big as me. To him, though, I'm just the team clown. But when he drags me into this graduation bet, it's no laughing matter. So why shouldn't this little cherub Gabe tutor me as well? In fact, I don't see why we can't share him in all *kinds* of ways. Seth is clearly a natural Daddy, Gabe thrives being doted on, and I'm happy to Daddy *and* be Daddied. Win-win, right?

GABE

Somehow, I've found myself standing up to the guy whose family pretty much owns Paddle Creek and put my neck on the line for two of the college's star players. Now we're spending every day together as I try and save their grades, and I don't know if I'm crazy but it's like they both *want* me. I've never had a boyfriend. I'm not even out to my overbearing parents. How could I choose between them…or do I actually have to when they *both* want to be my Daddies? After my life comes crashing down, it's their turn to come to my rescue. Maybe what me and these god-like men have isn't just a fling after all?

*Heaven Sent is a steamy, standalone MMM romance. It's the first book in the **Paddle Creek College** series, where it's always the quiet ones who get up to the best kind of trouble. This book features a geek tutoring two hot jocks, two hot jocks tutoring a geek in a completely different way, a trash panda with a heart of gold, a human ice cream sundae, a revenge curse, and a guaranteed HEA with absolutely no cliffhanger.*

Click here to get the Heaven Sent eBook

though, so in a way it's safe to flirt with him and see him lose that stiff upper lip. It's not like he'd be interested in me anyway if he ever discovered what I love wearing under my clothes. Tough guys like me shouldn't like satin and lace. They shouldn't want to feel pretty. But Sir makes me feel gorgeous, and I want to be *such* a good boy for him.

***Yes, Sir** is a steamy, standalone MM romance. It's the second book in the **Paddle Creek College** series, where it's always the quiet ones who get up to the best kind of trouble. This book features two people learning they don't have to be ashamed of who they are, a sassy brat who really wants to behave, a master in the bedroom who's a caring Daddy at heart, role playing so good it could win an Oscar, and a guaranteed HEA with absolutely no cliffhanger.*

Click here to get the Yes, Sir eBook

PADDLE CREEK #3: LITTLE PLEASURES BY HJ WELCH

One jaded Daddy. One brand new boy. A fake relationship that becomes all too real.

XANDER

It's bad enough I have to move back to Paddle Creek with my awful stepmom, but now my half-brother's best friend has decided he has to look after me—even pretending to be my new boyfriend for a family wedding to keep my stepmother off my back. What Ruben doesn't know is that I've been in love with him for as long as I can remember and spending so much time with him is torture. Until it isn't. I can't believe that he's interested in me and even wants to be my Daddy, unlocking something in me I never knew was there. But when my stepmom goes too far, can I rely on Ruben to be there for me seeing as no one else in my life ever has?

RUBEN

When my life-long best friend asks me to keep an eye on his half-brother, of course I agree. Except he's a young man now, not a kid, and he's tugging at every single one of my Daddy heartstrings. Xander has just moved back into town and between finishing his degree, part-time work, and hellish stepmother, he's stressing himself into knots. It's a long time since a boy interested me, but I just want to protect Xander from the whole world. No matter the cost.

*Little Pleasures is a steamy, standalone MM romance. It's the third book in the **Paddle Creek College** series, where it's always the quiet ones who get up to the best kind of trouble. This book features a Daddy introducing a boy to his inner little, the most loyal doggy best friend, a lot of dinosaurs, a heart-stopping rescue, and a guaranteed HEA with absolutely no cliffhanger. CW: Age play but no ABDL.*

Click here to get the Little Pleasures eBook

PADDLE CREEK #4: FOUR PLAY BY HJ WELCH

Three hungry wolves. One pretty little lamb. The hunt for love is on.

HARPER

I'm here for a good time, not a long time. When a total cutie asks me if I'd be interested in him and his two Daddies chasing me down and having their way with me, it sounds fun. I'm only in this crappy town for the summer, after all. But what we share is *intense.* I signed on to get caught…not to catch feels. However, when I find myself being hunted for real, can I really expect my wolf pack to come to the rescue?

RICK

After my husband and I swapped military life for married life, we quickly met our sweet baby boy who we'll do anything for. When Brady says he's found a sassy little lamb for the three of us to stalk, I'm happy to indulge him. But this broken young man swiftly captures all of our hearts, even though he says he can walk away any time. However, there's a difference between walking and being taken. Now I have the scent of a fool who's about to discover what happens when he's stolen what's *mine*.

Four Play is a super steamy, standalone MMMM romance. It's the fourth book in the **Paddle Creek College** series, where it's always the quiet ones who get up to the best kind of trouble. This book features exhilarating primal play, one hell of a paint ball match, an underwater themed motel, so many smooches, an obsessive ex-boyfriend, and a guaranteed HEA with absolutely no cliffhanger.

Click here to get the Four Play eBook

About the Author

Helen Juliet is a British author of contemporary MM fairy tale adaptations, including the international bestselling Beauty and the Beast retelling, Thorn in His Side. She lives just outside of London with her husband and three balls of fluff that occasionally pretend to be cats.

She began writing at an early age, later honing her craft online in the world of fanfiction on sites like Wattpad. Fifteen years and over half a million words later, she sought out original MM novels to read. By the end of 2016 she had written her first book of her own, and in 2017 she achieved her lifelong dream of becoming a full-time author.

When she's not writing she's usually dancing, singing, filming music videos, taking long walks, working on jigsaw puzzles, drinking prosecco, or talking about Eurovision.

She also writes contemporary American small town MM series as HJ Welch, including Pine Cove, Homecoming Hearts, and Paddle Creek College.

———

You can contact Helen Juliet via social media:

Newsletter (never miss a release!) – https://www. subscribepage.com/helenjuliet

Website (with FREE original stories) – www.helen-juliet.com

Facebook Group – Helen's Jewels

Facebook Page – @helenjulietauthor
Instagram – @helenjwrites
Twitter – @helenjwrites
Book Bub – @helenjuliet